# WISH YOU JOY

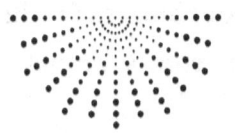

BOOKS BY JAN THOMPSON

CONTEMPORARY CHRISTIAN ROMANCE &
ROMANTIC WOMEN'S FICTION

**Savannah Sweethearts** (11 Books)
JanThompson.com/savannah

**Vacation Sweethearts** (5 Books)
JanThompson.com/vacation

**Seaside Chapel** (9-12 Books)
JanThompson.com/seaside

CHRISTIAN ROMANTIC SUSPENSE

**Protector Sweethearts** (6 Books)
JanThompson.com/protector

**Suspense Sweethearts Collection**
JanThompson.com/ss-vs-box

**Binary Hackers** (3 Books)
JanThompson.com/binary

# WISH YOU JOY

## SAVANNAH SWEETHEARTS BOOK 9

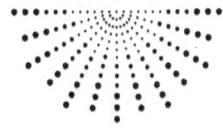

## JAN THOMPSON

Georgia
Press

WISH YOU JOY (SAVANNAH
SWEETHEARTS BOOK 9)

eBook Cover Design: Georgia Press LLC
Paperback Cover Design: Georgia Press and Deranged Doctor
Design

First eBook Edition: September 2016
ISBN: 978-1-944188-14-6

First Paperback Edition: February 2017
Paperback ISBN 978-1-944188-16-0

*To my Lord and Savior, Jesus Christ,*
*who died on the cross to save me from my sins*
*and rose again from the grave*
*to give me eternal life in heaven.*

*For God so loved the world,*
*that He gave His only begotten Son,*
*that whosoever believeth in Him should not perish,*
*but have everlasting life.*
—John 3:16

# ABOUT THE SAVANNAH SWEETHEARTS SERIES

## ELEVEN CHRISTIAN ROMANCES

From *USA Today* bestselling author Jan Thompson come these clean and wholesome Christian romances set on the romantic beaches of Tybee Island and in the coastal city of Savannah, Georgia, two of the most romantic coastal towns in the world.

Against a backdrop of ocean, sand, and sun, these inspirational novellas and novels showcase aspects of the human need for God and for one another. Have some tea, settle in a comfortable reading chair, and enjoy these sweet celebrations of faith, hope, and love in Jesus Christ.

PREQUEL TO SAVANNAH SWEETHEARTS, VACATION SWEETHEARTS, AND SEASIDE CHAPEL:

- Book 0: Ask You Later

WEI FAMILY:

- Book 1: Know You More
- Book 2: Tell You Soon

DUPREE FAMILY:

- Book 3: Draw You Near
- Book 4: Cherish You So

HOMETOWN FAMILIES:

- Book 5: Walk You There
- Book 6: Love You Always

PATEL FAMILY:

- Book 7: Kiss You Now
- Book 8: Find You Again

UNTERMEYER FAMILY:

- Book 9: Wish You Joy
- Book 10: Call You Home

Savannah Sweethearts Series Information:
JanThompson.com/savannah

Subscribe to Book News from Jan Thompson:
JanThompson.com/newsletter

# INTRODUCTION TO WISH YOU JOY

## SAVANNAH SWEETHEARTS BOOK 9

*The new CEO of Christmastown USA*
*celebrates Christmas year round.*
*His business partner*
*would rather not have Christmas at all.*

Christmastown USA has a new CEO. However, owning a majority share of the holiday-decorating company makes no difference for Cyrus Theroux if the other forty nine percent refuses to cooperate...

A year-round Christmas romance, *Wish You Joy* is Book 9 in *USA Today* bestselling author Jan Thompson's Savannah Sweethearts series of sweet, clean, wholesome, and inspirational contemporary Christian romances celebrating faith, hope, and love in Jesus Christ.

## CYRUS'S CHRISTMAS...

Whoopee! Christmastime is here again.

Cyrus is so excited that he is beside himself. Never mind that it's ninety three degrees outside in the middle of a hot July in Savannah. Christmas will be here any day now. He has checked his Christmastown USA warehouse twice, counted his inventory four times, and added ten new team members to join his thirty. He can spread them all over town. Sure, he can manage the decorating teams himself, even if his business partner can't handle it.

What's with Amy Untermeyer anyway? Maybe he should consider buying her share of the company. He will keep Mr. Untermeyer's memories and wishes alive. Yes, that's what he'll do. Kick Amy off the sleigh and keep Christmastown all to himself—

No.

There was something about Amy that draws Cyrus to her. Something he can't put his thumb on...


## AMY'S ANGST...

Christmas is too commercialized!

Amy simply cannot believe how anyone could

focus on the Christ of Christmas when people overspend and get stressed out at festivities they cannot enjoy with family members and relatives they do not wish to see or buy presents for.

Why Mom has given Amy only forty nine percent of Christmastown USA, she'll never know. Amy doesn't want it, but she can't sell it. To sell her share to some stranger would disrespect the memory of Dad, who inherited this business from Grandpa Earnest, who had started the company back in the fifties. The entire Untermeyer family lives from Christmas to Christmas. It was because of Christmastown that Amy's parents were able to send her and her two brothers to college.

Amy cherishes the happy memories of her childhood and the Untermeyer legacy until some devastating news makes her question everything she has ever known about the Untermeyer family...

Wish You Joy (Savannah Sweethearts Book 9):
JanThompson.com/wish

For book news, subscribe to Jan's mailing list:
JanThompson.com/newsletter

# PART I

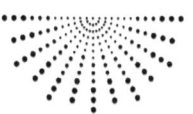

## PEACE

# CHAPTER ONE

"*L*et me get this straight." Cyrus Theroux splayed his fingers on the long worktable at one corner of the warehouse.

He glared at Mrs. Untermeyer's daughter, sitting across the table from him. Her back was facing the exit sign leading to the lobby and lunchroom.

Above them, the high ceiling of the cavernous warehouse loomed, waiting for the other shoe to drop.

Cyrus drew a deep breath, forming his next words cautiously. "I told you that Christmastown operates on a five-year business plan, but you just said you have no idea what you'll be doing in five months."

"I'm a destination wedding photographer, and I go where I get paid," Amy Untermeyer said.

"But five months from now, we're smack dab in the middle of Christmas."

Amy shrugged.

"It sounds—and looks—like you don't care about the company your grandpa started." Cyrus frowned as best he could to emphasize his point.

Well, maybe he shouldn't have played the emotion card, but the words had left his lips.

Amy remained seated. "I care, but Mom was supposed to run it, keep it in the family."

"In case you haven't noticed, your mother is up there in age, and she's got a bad hip and a couple of bad knees. She's been talking about moving to an assisted-living home."

Amy looked stunned, like that was new information to her.

Cyrus wondered if he should have said all that, but there it was. Those words had rolled out onto the battlefield and now faced this Goliath.

Amy looked like she didn't know how to respond.

Usually, Cyrus could read faces pretty well, but this time, he couldn't figure out which way the conversation was going, so he waited for Amy to make the next move.

She sat there. Stoic. Silent.

"Your mother said that her sons approved," Cyrus added.

Well, okay, bringing in Amy's brothers—one deployed in the Special Forces to places unknown, the other a chef on a cruise ship somewhere, and both who hadn't come home for Christmas in a few years—probably was a bad idea.

"My brothers?" Amy chuckled. "They don't care about Christmastown."

"And you do?"

*Ouch.* Cyrus quickly prayed for wisdom from God to shut his mouth *before* he snapped out another snide remark.

Still, it was true. Mrs. Untermeyer had said that while she had seen her sons once three years ago, this was the first time Amy had come home for a visit in five years. The fact that she was only here for a couple of days would make nary a difference in his business plan.

"Mrs. U sold me fifty-one percent of Christmastown last year. I've been running the company all this time, and we've been doing well. And now you show up." Cyrus straightened up. "You're dropping in for an inspection?"

"I was out of the country last Christmas, and I let it go. I thought I had time to discuss things with you. When Dad was running Christmastown, he didn't open for business until October. I didn't expect the warehouse to be operational in the summer."

"Well, this is how I run things, Miss Unter-meyer. I'm growing the company, and it's open year around." Just for good measure, Cyrus repeated it. "All. Year. Round."

"It's still July!" Amy said. "Christmas doesn't begin in July, in case you haven't heard. It doesn't even begin until after Thanksgiving."

"Says who? Some people put up a tree at the end of October."

"You do?" Amy asked.

"Aunt Marie wants it up by early November."

And Cyrus's uncle, Melvin Theroux, would do it for her sake, year after year. But this year, Uncle Mel was beginning to become as feeble as Aunt Marie.

Amy's face finally changed. "How's Marie?"

"She just turned eighty-six years old."

"No way."

"Uncle Mel is pushing ninety-five. Can you believe it?"

"Well,       he'd       always       looked wrinkly...pardon me."

Cyrus laughed. "Aunt Marie sometimes calls him her shar-pei. Woof!"

"Might be because he's out in the sun a lot in that nursery of his. Does he still have it?"

"He sold it to me." Cyrus stopped laughing. "And that's how it all began. Mrs. U was at the nursery, ordering poinsettias for Christmastown, when I was getting a tour of the tree farm next door."

Amy said nothing.

Cyrus wondered what was going through her mind. He wished he hadn't mentioned the tree farm.

He had wanted the Christmas tree farm as part of the sale of Christmastown, but Mrs. Untermeyer had held it back. Said her husband would have wanted her to keep maintaining it.

Cyrus would be more than happy to take over the tree farm.

It dawned on him that if Mrs. Untermeyer gave Amy the tree farm, his prickly business partner would suddenly have at least fifty-five percent of the shares of Christmastown.

*Yikes.*

*Time to put my guard up!*

The last thing he needed was to let Amy have leverage. He wanted to run Christmastown the way he wanted to run it. So there.

He studied the woman across the table. She still showed no emotions, except for that shrug earlier and her stunned look a bit later. He wondered how much he should say, and decided to summarize it, just in case she had some nefarious motives up her sleeves to reclaim or take over Christmastown.

There was no way he was going to let this world-traveling absentee daughter of Mrs. Untermeyer's snatch this proper business out of his hands.

"So in one fell swoop, you bought two businesses," Amy finally said.

"Struggling businesses. I could lose all my money." In retrospect, he shouldn't have sold his house in Atlanta, some stocks, and all of his inheritance money to pay for them.

He had done what he had learned not to in graduate school: put all his eggs into one basket.

Sometimes Cyrus wondered if Mrs. Untermeyer's whole reason of shaking up her family business was to bring her only daughter home to Savannah.

*Well, here she is.*

*Pretty she might be, but roses have thorns...*

"Look, I need this company to thrive," Cyrus said. "Or else I've lost all my investment."

"That's the problem. The love of money is the main reason gobs of companies have cannibalized Christmas!"

"You mean commercialized Christmas?"

"I said *cannibalized*. Did you want to speak for me?"

"Ah... No, ma'am. Sorry. Go on."

Cyrus felt slapped. Just because Amy looked like she was still in her twenties—at most, late twenties—compared to his early thirties, it didn't mean he could look down on her as being still a youth.

"Like I said, Christmas doesn't begin in July," Amy snapped. "Do you know it's 93 degrees outside today?"

Cyrus wanted to say something, but Amy waved her arms about.

He didn't have to turn around to know that she was pointing to the interior of the warehouse behind him, to the rows of shelves and boxes, the forklifts passing by them with more shipments from China. Fake Christmas trees that they could store year round.

"All these things represent the cannibalization of Christmas," Amy said above the noise of the passing forklift.

"Didn't your dad build this warehouse to replace an old one?"

"Yeah, but Christmas was never this commercialized when I was growing up."

"We all long for days gone by," Cyrus hissed.

"All? Not all."

"Are you correcting my words now? Speaking for me?" Cyrus tipped his head.

"Touché."

"We make a great pair—uh... Why did I say that?" Cyrus leaned back in his chair.

"They're just words." Amy seemed to brush him off. "The point is, Jesus wasn't even born in December, was He? Christmas is a commemorative season, not a real birthday holiday."

"I, for one, am glad we have a time of year to remember Jesus, who is my personal Lord and Savior. We have Christmas, and we have Easter."

"Don't get me started on Easter. Some say the word is derived from an old word for some spring goddess. Does that sound biblical to you?"

*Yikes. Where is this woman from?* "Don't you think we need to celebrate the death, burial, and resurrection of Jesus Christ?"

"Yes, but why don't we call it Resurrection Sunday instead of Easter Sunday?"

"We can," Cyrus said. "Others might not want to. It's their prerogative. But back to Christmas. Christmastown is a decorating business, and that has been the focus since your grandpa started the company back in the fifties, according to Mrs. U."

Now Amy was visibly moved.

Maybe it was because Cyrus had mentioned Grandpa Earnest. He wanted to test it again, but he'd better not. No point poking the rattlesnake when she was already riled up.

But it was time for him to end the meeting and get back to business.

"Miss Untermeyer, if you feel that strongly about un-Christmas, feel free to sell me your *minority* share of Christmastown," he said.

"Why should I? The memory of my dad is in Christmastown." Amy's shoulders slacked. She sank into the chair. Pointed here and there. "I used to come here with my brothers, and we'd skate up and down those aisles. Dad would be furious when he found us."

Cyrus turned his head to see where Amy was pointing. "It's dangerous to play in a working warehouse."

"We were teens."

"Yeah. I've been a stupid—strike that!—regular teen myself." Cyrus cleared his throat.

"You said it. I didn't. I was the one who always got into trouble with...with..."

Silence.

"Grandpa Earnest?" Cyrus took in a deep breath. "Tell you what. We just met each other when you walked in an hour ago. Let's just take it easy, and talk business another time."

"There's no other time. I'm gone in two days, remember?"

"When you come back then?"

"After Christmas."

"Wow." Cyrus prayed quickly for the right words. "You're not coming home for Thanksgiving and Christmas again?"

"Home? Savannah is Mom's hometown, not mine..."

Even as her words trailed off, Cyrus sensed some sort of nostalgia. And remorse, perhaps?

Amy sighed. "After Christmas I have some weddings to shoot in Auckland, then Rio."

"Auckland, as in New Zealand? Rio, as in Brazil?"

Amy nodded.

"All the way to the Southern Hemisphere?"

"That's where those places are, the last time I checked. It'll be warm-weather weddings in January. Your point, Cy?"

*Cy? She calls me Cy?*

*Nobody calls me Cy but my close friends...and Mom.*

"I'm sorry. You don't like to be called Cy," Amy said.

"Huh?"

"Your face just changed."

"What?"

"When I called you Cy."

"I just had a memory. That's all."

"Memory of?"

"Mom." Cyrus didn't know why he answered

her. It had been a private thought. *Oh well. It's out now.* "She called me Cy all the time."

"Called?"

"She passed away last year. She left me all her inheritance—I'm her only son—and I spent it all on Christmastown. It has to work, or I've failed big time." Cyrus straightened up. "Look, I'll be putting in a thousand percent of myself into this company, and I only have fifty-one percent of the profits. It seems to me that if you're going to leave after Christmas—or whenever—you're declaring that you're not doing your fair share."

"I have a job to get back to."

"Well, this is my job now. If you do nothing—or only one or ten percent—and I run the company all by myself when you're not here, it's hardly fair for you to get forty-nine percent of the profits."

Amy didn't reply, so Cyrus continued. "Sell me your share, and you can go free, back to your travels or whatever. I'll gladly do all the work here to keep Christmastown going."

Cyrus waited.

"You're not an Untermeyer," Amy finally said.

"And you know how to be one?"

As soon as Cyrus said those indicting words, Amy sprang up from her seat and strutted out of the noisy warehouse, leaving him sitting there, wondering what he had just done.

*S*ure enough, she had locked her keys in
the rental car.

Amy Untermeyer, an award-winning, world-
traveling wedding photographer who hadn't lost a
single luggage after millions of frequent flyer
miles...had now locked her keys in her car.

She could remain calm.

She could scream.

She could do both.

And embarrass the entire Untermeyer family.

Standing there in the two o'clock Savannah sun
in the middle of a humid July, droplets of sweat
forming on her forehead and neckline, and
surrounded by Christmastown company vans and
employee vehicles, Amy dug into her purse to find
her cell phone. Surely the rental-car company
could bring her a spare key.

And her cell phone was...

Dead.

Out of juice.

Some people said bad things happened in
threes, but Amy wasn't the superstitious kind. In
fact, she had learned at church—whenever she
could attend one in those various time zones she
ended up in—that superstition was an affront
to God.

Could God not do good things?

Could God not protect her?

Could God not let her walk back into the warehouse to ask that awful man for help?

Amy sighed.

*Pride, Amy. Pride.*

Amy knew, even as a little kid, that God hated pride. Grandpa Earnest had drilled that into his kids and grandkids, always quoting Proverbs 16:18.

"I know. I know," Amy said to no one. "'Pride goeth before destruction, and an haughty spirit before a fall.' See, I have it memorized, even, from the King James, Grandpa's favorite."

Her shoulders sagged.

*Humility or humiliation?*

Amy dragged herself back into the Christmastown warehouse, bracing herself to ask for help.

# CHAPTER TWO

"That was harsh, man." Rasheed Bolton shook his head.

He had been Cyrus's assistant for the past year. He had worked there for a while and knew the ins and outs of Christmastown.

In more ways than Cyrus could count, Rasheed was his right-hand man. He would've made the fifty-something man his vice president if Amy Untermeyer hadn't been in the way.

Rasheed spoke his mind, and it was one of his best qualities. He had insight into things. And people.

Yet today Cyrus disagreed with his employee—and deacon at his church. "Harsh? Business is business. Can't build a company on whiners."

"I'll take your word for it. I wasn't in the

convo." Rasheed checked off something on his iPad and opened up the next box in the new shipment that the forklifts had just brought into the warehouse.

Wreaths were in that box. All decorated.

Cyrus had ordered those himself. He knew exactly where they would go: onto the doors of every room at the Savannah Senior Living Resort. He was glad he had that chat with the resort director, Roger Patel, after church that Sunday when Uncle Mel couldn't attend. Cyrus had sat at the same table with Roger at Piper's Place, and over lunch they had hammered out Christmas.

Sure, it had been only April then, but like Cyrus had told Amy earlier, Christmastown operated year round.

"I'd give her a break, if I were you, Cy. The poor girl's mom sold a majority share of the family business to a stranger."

"Stranger? She's been away so long that her mom would've spent last Christmas alone had I not invited her to spend it with Aunt Marie and Uncle Mel."

"I hear you. Family is whoever is nearer to you."

*Nearer?*

Cyrus wondered if *closer* would have been a better word. He caught himself. Just minutes ago he had snapped when Amy corrected his words. Now he was doing the same to Rasheed.

If Rasheed wanted to use the word *nearer*, that was his choice.

*As for Amy...*

"She can take her emotional baggage elsewhere. I can't stand that type of woman. Always full of themselves. I pity the man who marries her."

Cyrus went to open the next box with a box cutter. As he stood up, there she was, standing maybe ten feet away, staring right at him.

Amy Untermeyer, the subject of his ugly comments.

*Uh-oh. How much did she hear?*

"May I use your phone?" Amy walked toward him. Her face was cold.

Very cold.

In this sort of Savannah heat, Cyrus felt a chill. He was certain she had probably heard his spiel. All of it.

"Pardon me?" Cyrus closed the box cutter and placed it on a rolling cart nearby.

Amy waved her phone. "My phone's out of juice. I need to make a phone call."

"Sure." Cyrus fished out his iPhone, entered his PIN code, and handed it to her.

"I'm going to need it for a bit."

"Whatever for?"

"I, uh, locked my keys in the car. I'm calling the rental-car place. They'll bring me another key."

Cyrus nodded. "My phone locks after a while, so maybe I should give you the PIN."

"You shouldn't trust me with it."

"After you're done, I'll change the number."

"Or you could just come with me, if you have time to spare—considering you do have all year."

"Half a year. That's all we have left!" Cyrus laughed, and he followed her out as though the piper had called him.

She walked fast, and he tried to keep up, all the while thinking that Amy had the prettiest walk he had ever seen this side of the world.

He wondered what it would take to keep up with a woman like her.

# CHAPTER THREE

"Twenty minutes? But you're at the airport. That's only nine minutes away to Pooler," Amy said on the phone to the person working at the rental-car company. "What? He's on break? All right. I'll wait."

She handed the phone back to Cyrus. "They're shorthanded. Twenty minutes."

"That'll be as much time as it takes to go to the airport and back. If you like, I can send someone—"

"No need. I'll just wait. I have all day, you know."

"You're funny."

"I am? Is that a compliment?" Amy didn't know why she bantered with him. "After that scathing remark about my love life, you're now complimenting me?"

Cyrus said nothing.

Amy suspected he was mulling over his own words.

*She can take her emotional baggage elsewhere.*

*I can't stand that type of woman. Always full of themselves.*

*I pity the man who marries her.*

"Speechless now, Mr. Theroux?" Amy said, then gasped. Her hand flung to her mouth. "I'm so sorry. If we keep cutting at each other, we'll destroy ourselves."

In the shade outside the front door of Christmastown, Cyrus's five o'clock shadow was a lighter brown. It had been darker under the fluorescent lights inside the warehouse.

They were standing close to each other, and Amy realized that he had big bones. The width of his shoulders was twice hers.

Why she had paid attention to his shoulders, she didn't know.

Cyrus still remained mum.

"Here you are, letting me use your cell phone, and I'm slicing and dicing at you with my speech."

Cyrus met her gaze.

"How about a truce?" Amy placed her hand on his thick arm.

*Whoa. He must lift weights.*

He just stood there.

Amy waved a hand in front of his face. "Please tell me you didn't fall asleep standing up."

Cyrus chuckled. "I was trying to figure out how to apologize to you for my own words."

"You were harsh, as your friend there said."

"You heard me all the way from that point?"

Amy nodded. "The warehouse echoes, don't you know? I could hear you all the way from the door. That is, when the forklifts were not moving around."

"It's like one big ear?"

"One big giant ear." Amy lifted her eyebrows. "It's very hard to insult me, Mr. Theroux, and make me feel the pinch. You did it twice in one afternoon. Bravo. Should I buy you coffee?"

"Maybe dinner?" Cyrus asked. "Oops. I don't know why I said that."

"Because you're brave and fearless."

"Or just dumb. I can be that sometimes."

"In front of girls especially? What would your girlfriend say?"

"I'm single."

"Ah. They all fled at the sight of you?"

Cyrus dug his fingers into his jean pocket. "You're pretty sharp tongued yourself, Miss Amy. How does your boyfriend put up with you?"

"We broke up."

It was hard to find a boyfriend while crisscrossing the globe looking for the best lighting and outdoor background for the perfect photography for her clients' destination weddings.

Ah, the perfect natural lighting, that elusive golden hour. It was something Amy and the best photographers in the world were always thinking about. When found, at the right time and place, the whole earth seemed to bask in a beautiful glow of diffused light.

That magic moment was tied to either the sunrise or the sunset.

Therein was Amy's problem.

Was there a Christian man who appreciated that God himself owned that golden hour?

Was there such a dude who would go with her anywhere to find that perfect shot?

Dad had gone with Mom back in their child-less days when Mom had been a working photographer. He would carry her heavy camera equipment for her. They would be out and about taking pictures of God's nature when Christmastown shut down for the year. Mom would later develop the film in the dark room that had once been in the basement of their family home.

Back in those predigital days.

Could Amy find a Christian boyfriend who loved the Lord and desired to please Him, someone like Dad?

*Very, very hard to find.*

*Okay. Impossible to find.*

"Oh sorry," Cyrus said. "I didn't mean to dredge up a heartache."

Amy shrugged. She realized she had been shrugging a lot lately.

However, life had thrown her some rotten eggs, and Cyrus here only reminded her of one more thing: losing Christmastown to someone outside the Untermeyer family was a testament of her lack of involvement in family affairs.

She should have called Mom more often.

Come home more often.

Then perhaps Mom would have thought of giving her the majority share of Christmastown instead of to this...this...

*Hunk?*

Melvin Theroux was a slight man, and no one in that family was big and brawny and built like a linebacker. Out of which tree did Cyrus fall? Maybe he inherited those features from his mom's side of the family. Or maybe there was a whole nonscrawny side of the Theroux family—

*Why in the world would I be curious about the Therouxes?*

And she knew the answer.

*It's this guy here.*

He was perhaps five or six inches taller than

she was in flats, and they would be at eye level with each other if she had worn her platform heels.

Why would it matter?

She had no idea.

"You shrug a lot," Cyrus said.

"Who's counting?"

"Here we go again. Let's see who wins the sniping contest."

"Oh, I'll win. Hands down."

"Is that a swipe at me?" Cyrus asked.

Amy almost shrugged, but she stopped. She could feel her shoulders gunning for it. She coughed a little.

"I'm keeping an eye on you, Miss Untermeyer." Cyrus then lifted his chin in the direction of the street. "That looks like your knight in shining armor, bringing you the spare key."

The little half-a-car rolled into the parking lot.

Amy waved to the driver, who then brought the car up against the curb.

"Well, thank you, Cy—Cyrus—for hanging out with me here while I waited for my rescuer," Amy said.

Cyrus slapped his forehead. "We should've waited inside. It would've been cooler."

"We were too busy cutting each other down to notice."

"And we didn't get our coffee."

"There wouldn't have been enough time to get to a café." Amy opened the passenger-side door of the little car. To the driver, she said, "Thanks for coming. My car is over there, two rows away."

"I was going to take you to the lunchroom." Cyrus pointed to a bank of windows behind him. "Coffee on the house."

"Ah, you're cheap too." Amy laughed as she got into the car and shut the door.

# CHAPTER FOUR

"*I*'m not cheap." Cyrus nearly slammed the door to his office. It swung wide. The hinges creaked.

"Yes, you are." Rasheed's voice coming behind him could not be at a worse time.

"What? You taking her side now?" Cyrus walked to his metallic desk, piled up with bills and invoices and sketches of patent-pending inventions for Christmastown. No hope of getting those past Amy Untermeyer.

Rasheed sat down on an old office chair, circa 1950, across from the desk. "I see her point of view. She doesn't want Christmastown to be a run-of-the-mill holiday decorating company."

"It's not."

"It is too if you keep outsourcing overseas. That

new shipment of wreaths that came in today—well, they look like any other cheap dollar store wreaths, if you take a second look."

"Local products are expensive."

"Specialize, then. Be different." Rasheed crossed his legs, his work boots clean and polished. "Have some class. Style."

"It costs more."

"So be it. It'll weed out the riffraffs, and we can go for customers who are willing to pay for quality."

Cyrus leaned back against his old armchair, which Mrs. Untermeyer used to sit in, and stared at the ceiling. He spotted a dry stain. Water damage. He'd had that fixed last fall. Cost him a pretty penny.

There was a reason this company had been struggling.

Maybe it had been a mistake to buy it.

*Stupid me.*

Cyrus wondered what life might have been like had he remained in Atlanta and kept working at the warehouse there. He'd had a wonderful supervisor job with great pay and benefits, though he had always known that he was cut out for more than middle management.

Like being the CEO of his own company.

*Just not a seasonal decorating business like*

*Christmastown.*

He had no connections to the Untermeyer legacy, no ties to their memories. Nothing. He had looked at Christmastown from purely a business standpoint.

But if he couldn't get Amy on board, her forty-nine percent clout would drag the entire company down.

"You have to agree that the meaning of Christmas can be lost in the festivities," Rasheed said.

Cyrus opened his eyes. "Festivities? You wanted to say money-making schemes?"

"Stop putting ideas in my mind." Rasheed laughed. "But now that you mentioned it, yes, I do believe I would have said that—had my mama not taught me to be polite in front of people."

"Bless her heart. How is she doing?"

"She's living it up at the Resort. Has a new boyfriend and all. I'm scared for her. All that action and activities might not be good for her heart."

Cyrus smiled. "Well, we've got a contract to decorate that entire place after Thanksgiving. Gave them a discount. That should spread some Christmas cheer."

"And bring you into the good, charitable graces of one Amy Untermeyer?"

"I wish." Cyrus groaned. "I just met her this morning, and already we had a fight this afternoon. If she's not on board with our company goals, she's going to sabotage everything I've worked for the last year. What do I do, Rasheed?"

"That is a great question to ask God, Cy." Rasheed tapped the armrests. "As your deacon, I urge you to pray before you speak to Amy again."

"What if God takes time to answer me?"

"God's timing is always perfect."

"Amy leaves town in two days."

"Then you better get moving. Whatever it is that's exploding between the two of you, you'd better get it resolved. Hearing the two of you duke it out, it sounded like a married couple bickering."

Thing was, Cyrus didn't know how to resolve this conflict. He planned to pray, but what would he ask God for? What if God decided to side with Amy? What if God allowed Christmastown to shut down? He would never get his money back.

"It's July already," Rasheed added. "I don't know how you two will survive until Christmas."

"If Amy gets her way, there will be no Christmas."

"Have you offered to buy her out?"

"Tried. Didn't work." Cyrus was surprised at the guttural sound that came out of his own throat. "She's hanging on to something she hadn't bothered to preserve the last ten years the company had been shrinking and losing money. She gave me the impression she doesn't care if the company goes under as long as it stays in the Untermeyer family."

"I find it hard to believe she's that anti-Christmas."

"I'm not overreacting."

"Maybe if you get to know her a bit more..."

"You mean get into the viper's pit with her and let her tear me to shreds?"

"Love covers sins." Rasheed swiped his tablet, cleared his throat, and read aloud. "'Hatred stirreth up strifes: but love covereth all sins.' Proverbs 10:12. That's worth memorizing."

"Is this a recruiting tool, Rasheed? You want me to attend your Sunday school class?"

"The door is always open. We meet downstairs next to the engine room." Rasheed lifted a finger. "But that's not until Sunday. Meanwhile, you have all week with a problem in your hands."

"And only two days to solve it." Cyrus drew a deep breath and dropped his forehead onto his messy desk. Something snapped, and suddenly he realized he had to remake that prototype pop-up mini wreath.

As if on cue, the wreath popped open, and a toy soldier sprung out and poked him in the eye.

"Owwww!"

# CHAPTER FIVE

*O*nce upon a time, Christmas had been Amy's favorite time of the year. She could see the film reel in her mind, those happy days of working after school at Dad's Christmastown warehouse in Pooler, a town outside Savannah. She could see her own cheerful face as she hauled Christmas trees and wreaths and decorations into the company truck and accompanied both parents from hotel to restaurant to museums to historic homes, decorating for Christmas.

Year after year, season after season, until...

Amy sniffed.

She wiped her eyes on the sleeves of the blouse and willed herself to get out of the rental car. She leaned against the door, standing there between the car and the interior wall of Mom's garage. The garage door was open to the afternoon sun, the humid air gushing into the space around her.

She didn't move.

*I'm sorry, Dad.*

She should have gone with Dad that evening. He'd had to work all night and had been short-handed when two of the Christmastown employees came down with the flu. But she had a paper to write for class and assignments to complete, so she had begged off going with him.

It was the same night Mom had gone to Atlanta to visit relatives.

It still annoyed Amy to think that those relatives had been more important than helping Dad in the business.

*Oh, the hypocrite that I am, I can't cast the first stone at Mom.*

Amy's own schoolwork at college had been more important than helping Dad.

In the end, Dad had to do most of the work himself that night.

That fatal night.

The police had said that he never saw the tractor-trailer coming across the median.

For nine years Amy had chosen to believe that Dad had died instantly in the multivehicle pileup. The driver of the big, old truck had fallen asleep at the wheel, in the middle of the night on Interstate 95.

She breathed in deeply and found herself standing in Mom's empty kitchen. She did not remember putting the key into the kitchen door. Then again, Mom had a bad habit of not locking any of her doors.

The afternoon sunlight filtered in through sheer curtains, and there were soft shadows on the kitchen floor, shadows of the outside—of trees, leaves, branches of the old oak tree that Amy knew well, the same tree that had been part of her happy childhood, breezy days of summer when she had swung back and forth on an old wooden swing under the tree.

More memories than Amy cared to remember.

"Mom?"

No response.

Mom's car was in the garage, so she had to be somewhere. Perhaps she was upstairs taking a nap?

Amy glanced at her watch. Three o'clock!

How could it be three already?

And then she spotted cookies in a jar. Mom always surprised her with cookies of some sort. She lifted the glass lid. Shortbread cookies! Yum!

Munching down one, then another, and another, Amy made her way to the living room with a paper napkin stacked with cookies, looking for Mom. She was nowhere to be found. On a side table in the living room, something buzzed.

It was Mom's pink cell phone.

It buzzed again.

Out of curiosity, Amy pressed the round button. A text message became visible.

*No! I don't want to see her.*

*She doesn't need to know.*

*Let me die in peace.*

Just as Amy noticed that the sender was Walt —Uncle Walt?—her own phone rang.

She put the cookies down on the coffee table in the living room.

It was a phone call from her personal assistant at Amy's Destination Photography. Daisy usually traveled with one of Amy's two photography teams. She was calling from Mykonos, where they were doing a photo shoot for a bridal magazine.

"That doesn't work, Daisy," Amy said as calmly as she could into her iPhone. "I can't fly from Kyoto to Aberdeen, set up the shoot, and be ready for the dress rehearsal in eight hours. Are you kidding me?"

She plopped onto a plush couch. Listened for a bit.

"I'm glad you're fixing this schedule snafu." Amy tried not to show how irritated she was.

This wasn't the first time Daisy had messed up

her schedule. It cost money to change flights and switch hotels, but more importantly, it was a nightmare to make it all happen without the clients knowing that she almost missed the weddings.

Memories of weddings. Those were what ADP specialized in recording. Amy's film crew was par excellence, but Amy was the only one of two full-time photographers at her company. With Daisy's crazy scheduling, Amy was worn out.

She stifled a yawn.

The afternoon wore on as Daisy droned apologetically.

Amy nodded, not at Daisy on the phone, but because her head was heavy. Tired. Sleepy.

"I guess that could work. Send Midori to Aberdeen then. I'll handle the Kyoto wedding this Saturday. What's after that?" She waited. "Okay. Fine. I'll go to Denali in Midori's place next week. Send the crew ahead of me?"

Amy checked the updated schedule on her app. She didn't like to look over Daisy's shoulder, but what could she do? Her company's reputation was at stake. Too many times she had hired freelance photographers at the last minute because of overbooking or overlapping schedules. Those photographer friends of hers were only too happy to help her out—for a price.

It took all her time to keep her photography

business going enough to make ends meet, pay the bills, and pay herself a salary. Stretched too thin as she was, with jet lag to boot, she couldn't possibly take on anything else.

*Oh.*

She      couldn't      handle      Christmastown, could she?

# CHAPTER SIX

Two days. Cyrus had two days to convince Amy that he wasn't cheap—

Cheap?

Uh, no. That wasn't why he was here, standing in front of Mrs. Untermeyer's front door, waiting for a girl to say yes to his proposal.

Business proposal.

Cyrus wiped his sweaty palms on his jeans. He lifted his tee shirt to his nose, praying it didn't smell too bad after a drive over here in Uncle Mel's old Grand Marquis whose air conditioner had given out.

He felt nervous, suddenly self-conscious. He was sure Amy was going to laugh at him. Did she even need a reason to laugh at him?

*What on earth am I doing?*

He made an about-turn and in no time at all, he was stepping off the porch and heading back to the car.

"So you ring the doorbell to people's houses and run off?" Amy's voice hit Cyrus like a censure.

Perhaps he shouldn't have taken it that way. He had, indeed, come to see her uninvited.

He turned around. Amy was munching some cookies.

"Want some? They're shortbread, but I think Mom threw in some coconut."

And just like that, the ice broke.

Then Amy said, "Mom's not here."

"Uh, I'm here to see you," Cyrus said, standing at the bottom of the steps. He had prayed for wisdom, but he was still unsure of how to approach Amy. He wanted to be transparent with her. Show her who he really was. Gain her trust to run Christmastown.

Why her endorsement mattered, he had no idea.

"I brought you a peace offering," Cyrus said.

"I can't be bought."

"Bribed?"

"Never." A grin crept up her face. "Unless it's food."

"You just ate cookies."

"Meaning what?"

39

"How many did you eat?"

"Why would you care?"

"Any left for me?"

"It depends." Amy crumpled the paper napkin in her hand.

"Depends on what?"

"Your peace offering."

"What peace—oh yes. One sec." Cyrus popped the trunk of Uncle Mel's car. He lifted the brown cardboard box with *Christmastown* written all over it, and hauled it up to the porch.

"What's inside?" Amy asked, her eyebrows furrowing.

"We can open it here."

"It's too hot outside." Amy held the door open. "The AC is on in the living room."

"Okay." Cyrus walked past her, once again afraid she'd smell his sweat and fear and trepidation. He put the box down on the wood floor of the living room.

"Let it be known that Cyrus Theroux has brought me a peace offering," Amy said.

At first Cyrus didn't know how to respond. Then he felt amused at the side of Amy he hadn't known before. How could he have known? They had only met that day.

"I am concerned that we're the only ones in

this house right now," Amy said. "Unless Mom's upstairs napping or online."

*I like that honesty.* "Next time, I'll bring Ted."

"Ted?"

"My golden. He's nine and has arthritis."

"Poor doggie."

"Yes. He's very needy. Lots of TLC needed. Like me..." Cyrus coughed.

"Let it be known that Cyrus has confessed. The Christmastown CEO—a nonfamily member who now owns fifty-one percent of my grandpa's company—has confessed to being needy."

Cyrus stared at her.

*What in the world?*

*Did Mrs. U spike the cookies?*

"What's in the box?" Amy asked, seemingly ready to move on.

Cyrus's eyes lit up as he started to open the box. He nearly leapt to his feet, he was so buoyant.

"It's not Christmas morning yet, Cy," Amy said quietly.

"It feels like it with that AC turned so low."

"Let it be known that I'm dealing with an overgrown kid," Amy said nonchalantly.

"Why do you talk like that, all of a sudden?" Cyrus asked.

"Like what?"

"All these *let it be known* stuff."

Amy sighed and retreated to a couch. "You came here for something. Get on with it, please? I need to get some rest."

"I'm not your enemy, Amy." Cyrus stood next to the box.

"You could have texted me that."

"Your mom and I get along very well."

"Good for her."

"So I figured—"

"I'm not her."

Cyrus waited. Had to change his tactic. Perhaps it was time to give it to her plainly. "Look, we can't run Christmastown if we can't have decent conversations, partner to partner."

"I agree."

"You do?"

Amy nodded. "I think the whole business arrangement is ridiculous."

"Your mom says you don't have time to run Christmastown. That's why I'm here."

"She said what?"

Cyrus lifted a palm. "You can trust me with the company. I'll make you proud, Miss U."

"Miss U?" Amy lifted her eyebrows. "It was Amy, and now it's Miss U?"

"I take that back. I won't *miss you* at all when you go back to your work out there in the wild blue yonder." Cyrus was a bit worried when Amy didn't react.

"Why do you think Mom sold you such a large chunk of our family business?" she asked.

"You'll have to ask her. All I know is that she can't do this anymore. When she had her knee replace—"

"What? When?" Amy sat straight up.

"You didn't know?"

"Would I have asked you if I did?"

"Yeah. Okay. It was in the fall of last year. Don't worry. Our church helped."

"Your church? Or you go to the same church?"

"Yes. I'm checking out a new singles Sunday school class this Sunday. You're welcome to sit in with—oh, I forgot. You're flying out Wednesday, right?"

"Right. It's hard to go to church out there, but I do listen to Pastor Flores online whenever I can."

"Maybe someday you'll be in town on a Sunday morning, and you can come to church with us."

"Us?"

"I usually pick up your Mom around eight o'clock, but lately she has another ride."

"Who picks her up now?"

"Her boyfriend." Cyrus was about to peel back

the top of the box, when he heard a shriek from Amy.

"Mom has a boyfriend?" Amy's voice rose.

Cyrus wasn't sure how to respond. Had Amy been so out of touch with her own family? He decided that traveling around the world was over-rated if she couldn't be with her family.

Then again, she might not want to be with her family.

And why would anyone distance herself from her own family?

*What's wrong with Amy?*

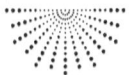

# CHAPTER SEVEN

"*A*re you ready?" Cyrus asked.

Amy had never seen anyone so excited about a brown cardboard box.

"I don't know, Cy. A pop-up tree sounds like..." *Failure.*

"I don't want to fill in the blanks. You think it's cheap."

"Cheap? That's a word too."

"How can you say that if you've never seen it?" Cyrus raised his big palms before Amy could say another word. "Please hold all your questions until the end of the demo. Thank you."

Amy folded her arms and leaned back into the couch. And waited.

"For the record, I'm not cheap. Christmas should be fun."

"I get that."

"You do?"

"What's that supposed to mean?" Amy asked.

"See, there we go again. You know what the Bible says? 'But if ye bite and devour one another, take heed that ye be not consumed one of another.'"

"Pastor Flores preached that last Sunday. Galatians 5:15. I heard it on my phone app."

"Well, good. And just so you know, I was there in church, taking notes. If it makes you feel more confident about who I am, I am a churchgoing believer, and I have to answer to God for my stewardship over my job, my family, my life."

"What are you saying? That I can trust you to run Christmastown?"

Cyrus nodded.

"A man with a cardboard box."

"It's what's inside that matters."

Amy laughed.

"You just laughed at me."

"With you, Cy."

"Do you see me laughing?" Still standing, Cyrus leaned toward Amy. He pointed at the corner of his left eye. "Look. A tear is coming out."

"A tear of shame?"

Cyrus moaned—it sounded like a moan—and

sat down in an armchair. He buried his face in his hands. "I tried, Lord."

He closed his eyes, leaned way back, and stretched his long, long legs in front of him.

Amy felt bad as she sat there looking at that man with the sad face.

*What have I done?*

Amy crossed the floor and touched Cyrus's shoulder. He jerked back.

"I'm sorry," Amy said.

"I'd better go." Cyrus tried to get up, but Amy was in his way. "Please step aside."

"I'm sorry." Amy didn't move.

Cyrus didn't reply.

"That verse is a good reminder for us," Amy said.

Cyrus grinned.

"We have been devouring each other all day long." Amy hesitated, then continued. "You were right."

Cyrus's grin broadened. "What? Say again?"

Then and there, Amy knew that Cyrus was the kind of person who didn't bear grudges for long.

She wondered what else she should find out about him.

"Show me your pop-up tree," Amy said.

"Yes, ma'am." Cyrus made his way back to the cardboard box.

Amy walked next to him. "Does it come with a remote?"

"We could certainly add that feature." Cyrus smiled, his eyes bright and...so endearing.

Amy said nothing more, praying that her thoughts would be reined in. Cyrus was her business partner, and that was that. They could probably be business associates, perhaps, but no more than that.

Cyrus stepped toward the box. "I have to tell you something."

"Uh-oh."

"This box arrived this afternoon, and I haven't seen what's inside."

"No kidding."

"So we'll discover together."

"Fun."

"Literally, or is that an insult?"

Amy frowned. "Take it at face value."

"Okay. Ready?" Cyrus asked.

Amy nodded.

Cyrus lifted the green, leafy cube out of the box. It looked like a compressed geometric wreath. It certainly didn't look anything like a Christmas tree.

Cyrus placed the cube on the floor. He turned it here and there, and somehow pressed something.

Amy waited.

And waited.

"Come on!" Cyrus pressed the hidden button again. Multiple times. "Pop up!"

Still, nothing happened.

Absolutely nothing.

If Amy could describe Cyrus's face, the word for it would be *devastated*.

Devastated.

Destroyed.

As for the pop-up Christmas tree, it was a dud.

*A total dud.*

# CHAPTER EIGHT

*A*round eleven o'clock at night, Amy was awoken by the doorbell ringing, door slamming, door bolting, and door alarm being set. It was all about doors.

*Arrrggghh!*

She buried her head under the pillow and tried to resume her sleep.

It would not come.

She sighed, rolled out of bed, and dragged herself out of the guest bedroom. Yes, she had been sleeping in the guest bedroom upstairs because her childhood bedroom downstairs had been turned into Mom's photography studio, which hadn't been used for years, and was now a home office of some sort.

Therein was the irony.

Mom had been—probably still was—a very good photographer with a better sense of timing than Amy had. Perhaps someday the Lord would call them to do some joint projects together. Until then, they would not be doing anything together, in spite of the fact that Mom had taught Amy everything she knew about photography.

Mom was sitting at the breakfast nook and thumbing through what looked like old photographs.

"It's late, Mom." Amy slid into the seat on the other side of the pine table.

Mom nodded.

She ran her freckled fingers across the photographs and turned the page.

"You left your phone at home," Amy said.

For a moment, Mom froze in midmovement. Amy noticed but said nothing when Mom moved on to the next page in the old album.

"Whatcha looking at?" Amy asked.

"Your childhood."

"This late at night?"

Mom said nothing.

"You can probably see better in the daytime when the sun is shining."

"I can see just fine."

"I'm not telling you what to do. Just suggesting."

Mom closed the album. Placed both palms on it. "It was so long ago."

"What was?"

"Everything."

"Sometimes the past catches up to you."

"What are we talking about, Mom?" Amy wondered if it had anything to do with that text message from Walt. She could not be sure it was Uncle Walt. She couldn't begin to presume what went on in Mom's life.

She had been away too long to feel a connection to her mother, a rapport of any kind.

This last big thing Mom had done last year—bringing Cyrus into Christmastown—had rubbed Amy the wrong way. She still hadn't gotten any explanation from Mom about it. Why had she done it?

"I miss your dad." Mom's voice was so low that Amy could barely hear it.

"I miss him too." Amy reached across the table and gently placed her palm on top of Mom's clasped hands.

"If he were alive, we wouldn't have to sell half of Christmastown to Cyrus."

Amy nodded, the years of unspoken words contracting into that moment in time when understanding dawned. Mom could no longer handle a business. She was tired, weary. And Amy had been no help.

"Have you heard from Garrett or Isaac?" Mom asked.

"Not lately."

"Wish I knew where Isaac is now on that world cruise."

"You could always google." Amy shook her head. "Some life he's leading. He emailed me eight or nine months ago, saying that he has a whole team of chefs with him, and while he enjoyed being the chef de cuisine cooking for five thousand people each night, at some point he's going to get tired of it all."

"Wish we had someone cooking for us!"

"I agree!"

"And Garrett?"

"Not a word. Incommunicado for a while. We can pray that God will keep him safe."

Mom nodded. "I didn't want him to join the Special Forces, but he was stubborn."

And therein was the second realization in Amy's head.

Mom was alone.

She lived alone.

*May it never be that she dies alone.*

"So you leave on Wednesday?" Mom asked. Her voice cracked.

Amy nodded, measuring her words. "My able assistant has messed up my schedule again. I'm paying a contract photographer extra now so we can be everywhere at the same time. I hope to be back in November."

"For Thanksgiving?" Mom sounded hopeful.

How could she disappoint Mom now?

"Yes, that's my plan." *My new plan.*

"Are you getting enough food and rest, traveling everywhere?" Mom asked.

No and no. "I try."

"You don't like the jet lag. You told me."

"I hate it."

"Then why do it?"

"It's a job."

"If you don't enjoy your job—I should never have gotten you into photography, dear."

"No, no. I love the work itself, but not the traveling. I don't know how long I'm going to be able to live out of suitcases." Amy shifted on the bench. "Some days I want to just open a photography studio somewhere and stay put."

"You do?"

Amy nodded. "We'd better get some sleep. I have an early meeting with Cyrus."

"How are you getting along with him?" Mom stood and picked up the album, cradling it in her arms, close to her chest.

Amy wondered again if Mom was reminiscing something triggered by the text message she had received from a certain Walt.

"Famously. He's like a big kid. He came over here this afternoon and pranced around a Christmas tree box."

"Was it a pop-up tree?"

Amy laughed. "He said it was, but the pop-up part didn't work. He was so mad. I was too, for Christmastown's sake. He's going to the factory in the morning to straighten it out. Give them the *what's what*."

"He's been working on that for a year. Has patent pending and all."

"Is that right?"

"Let the man dream, Amy."

Amy hadn't pegged Cyrus as a dreamer, but the man had vision. She hadn't met anyone else who lived and breathed Christmas besides Dad. Cyrus could come close if he kept on inventing Christmassy things.

*Let the man dream.*

# CHAPTER NINE

*W*ith great reluctance, Amy let Cyrus drag her halfway across the state of Georgia to Macon, where his great investment was. Amy hoped he hadn't put the rest of his fortune into it.

Tuesday morning turned out to be a beautiful day for a drive into the country, and it was easy to get to Macon from Savannah.

*Just get on Highway 16, and keep driving. Hang a left, and there you are.*

They had taken a Christmastown van because Cyrus wanted to bring home about a dozen trees for some volunteers from church to test.

If it worked, Cyrus would be a genius.

If it failed, Christmastown's reputation would

never be the same again. They might as well have called it Christmasclown.

They hadn't said much to each other on the drive. Amy was on her iPhone most of the time, correcting Daisy's scheduling fiascos. Cyrus was listening to some hymns, learning new ones, it seemed.

It was just as well they hadn't said much to each other. Amy didn't know what they could talk about. They were utter strangers.

Amy swiped her iPhone and groaned. "Aarrgh!"

"Whassup?" Cyrus asked.

"Another destination wedding canceled."

"A what wedding?"

"Never heard of it?" Amy sat up. Adjusted her seat belt.

"Sorry. I live under a rock."

"Or under a coconut shell."

"Never seen a live one."

Amy laughed. "Coconut shells are not live."

"No? Not like a seashell?"

"You're pulling my leg, Cy."

"Made you feel better, didn't I?"

"Clever elf, you."

Cyrus nearly slammed on his brakes. "Did you just evoke a word that's heard at Christmastime?"

"Secular Christmas-speak. Ignore at will." Amy sighed as she returned to her iPhone. "Ah, the bridegroom bailed. Didn't want to be married at Mount Fuji."

"Isn't that an active volcano?"

"Well, it hasn't erupted in a few hundred years. Thing is, my entire crew has bought plane tickets. We've booked hotels. It's going to cost us a bundle."

"Deposits?"

"Yeah. No refund for them. Still, that's money lost. Six months of planning up in smoke."

"Better for them to cancel the wedding than to cancel their marriage."

"You mean divorce later?"

"Makes sense for them to be absolutely sure before they go through with a wedding." Cyrus leaned back against the vinyl headrest.

"Absolutely?"

"Why not? To me, a wedding to the love of my life is a point of no return."

"The love of your life?"

"Who else would I marry?" Cyrus chuckled. "But no destination anything for me."

"Not even for the honeymoon?" Amy asked.

"There are plenty of places to see in the United States you can drive to. Why fly?"

"Well, you could drive to Canada and Central America, but you're going to need a passport."

"I'll just stay in the USA."

"Cyrus." Amy turned toward him.

"What?"

"Do you even have a passport?"

After a pause, Cyrus responded, "No need."

"You don't have a passport."

"I'm happy where I am."

"Don't you want to see the world?"

"I can google. Or watch YouTube videos. Or TV. Plenty to see."

"Not the same as in person, Cy." Amy had never met a person who didn't want to see places for himself—places outside the United States.

"I don't fly."

"Seriously?"

Cyrus nodded. "My ears hurt the last time I flew."

"When was that?"

"I was four."

"And you're how old now?"

"Thirty-two. Why?"

"Let me get this straight. For twenty-eight years you haven't gotten on an airplane," Amy said.

"I prefer trains."

"You can't take a train to England or Europe or Asia, at least not in the present day. I suppose you could travel on ships."

"Not sure if I can do ships. Motion sickness."

Cyrus slowed down the van to merge into a lane. "Besides, I've been too busy. For the last year, I've spent all my time increasing revenues for Christmastown."

"No vacation?" Amy was surprised.

"No time. And if I do, it's staycation for me."

"You're going to burn out."

"Then you can buy me out."

"No need, Cy. You'd be dead from exhaustion, and I'll take over the company."

Cyrus chuckled. "I can't imagine what you're going to do with it."

Amy wondered too. How could she run Christmastown and Amy's Destination Photography at the same time?

"I have to make it work, Amy. Christmastown is all I have."

"Not true, Cy. You have God, family."

"My parents are deceased. My aunt and uncle are having serious health problems. It's a matter of time before I'll be alone."

"Don't say that."

There was silence between them as traffic, entering the city of Macon, slowed in front of their van. It was almost lunch hour, and they hadn't made any plans.

"How about lunch on the way to the factory?" Cyrus asked.

Amy sensed he was trying to change the subject. *Okay. I'll bite.* "Sure. Know any good place to eat around here?"

"We'll find a restaurant with a full parking lot."

"That works."

# CHAPTER TEN

"What broke the ice between us?" Cyrus asked as they waited at their restaurant booth for their southern fried chicken to arrive.

It was funny to him that they had both ordered fried chicken. It had been even more intriguing to find out Amy loved fried chicken just as he did.

"The Christ in Christmas?" Amy offered.

"Of course. Only Him." Cyrus slurped his iced tea through a straw. "It's my turn to apologize for being difficult to talk to yesterday."

"You? It was me. I wasn't being a team player."

"You? I was playing hard to please."

"So we're all sinners saved by grace." Amy squeezed another slice of lime into her iced tea.

"Did you realize that we both drink iced tea through a straw?"

Cyrus nodded.

Amy frowned. "How did Mom decide to sell Christmastown to you? I know you said that you met her when y'all were at the poinsettia nursery at the same time."

"You know, I'm wondering about that. Did Uncle Mel and Mrs. U plan something we didn't know?"

"Beats me."

"Shall we ask them?" Cyrus tilted his head, like he often did when he was deep in thought.

"I doubt if we'd get a straight answer."

"But?"

"But I'm curious," Amy said. "Aren't you?"

"For sure. We started out yesterday on the wrong foot, but today we find out we have too many uncanny things in common."

Just then their fried chicken platters arrived.

"Exhibit A." Amy pointed.

"There's a slight difference. You like yours spicy, and I like mine plain."

"Close enough, Cy."

"Right." And he didn't mind Amy calling him Cy. In fact, he rather liked it. And why would that be? Perhaps it was because they had started to become friends.

The Word of God had chastised them and brought them to a common understanding. They were not of unequal yoke anymore as business partners once they yielded to the teaching of God.

Galatians 5:15 came to his mind again.

*But if ye bite and devour one another, take heed that ye be not consumed one of another.*

"Tell me what you do for yourself at Christmas," Amy suddenly asked.

"What do you mean?" Cyrus didn't want to assume, though he could take a wild guess regarding where Amy was going with the question.

"You do much for others. When you get home to your house, what do you have there?"

"This year I'm going to have a pop-up Christmas tree."

"That works." Amy laughed.

"Yes, that works." Cyrus reached across the table. Then realizing what he was about to do, he pulled back his hand. "Would you like to say grace?"

"You say it. Please?"

And so Cyrus did, thanking God for their fried chicken, praying that their business would thrive and bring glory to God, and mentioning that he was glad Amy could stay for another week in town.

After they said *amen,* Cyrus decided that this was as good a time as any to find out more about

Amy. But first, the chicken. He dug in to his still-steamy chicken leg quarters.

They ate in silence for a while, refilling their iced tea.

"How do you celebrate Christmas while traveling?" Cyrus asked when they were almost done eating the greasy chicken.

"Sometimes I don't. It depends on what country we're in. In many countries, Christmas is part of the holiday landscape. In fact, it's a big sales event. However, in some countries where Christianity is frowned upon, you don't see Christmas as a big event. I tend to go to resorts, since we're shooting destination weddings, and almost everywhere we go, Christmas happens."

"But?"

"You seem to know that I'm not telling you everything."

"Right."

"I'm not fond of people getting married on Christmas day because it takes the focus—shifts it —from Christ to the wedding itself. It's like people who were born on Christmas day getting their limelight shadowed by Christ's birth."

"I hear you. But?"

"I needed the income. So if they wanted to get married on the beach in Tahiti on Christmas day, and my team had no problem showing up, then we'd go for it." Amy wiped her hands.

"You spoke in past tense. Something changed?"

"Like you said yesterday, Mom is not getting any younger," Amy explained. "Last night I found her looking over some old photos."

She leaned against the table. "And I saw a text message from someone named Walt. It could be Uncle Walt. Oh, you probably don't know him."

"No, I don't." Cyrus pushed his empty plate away.

"Mom went out and forgot her phone. It was on a side table in the living room. I heard a buzz. The message was right there, on the center of the screen."

Cyrus figured she pushed the button to read the message. "I don't want to know what it says."

"It says someone named Walt is dying."

"I just said I don't want to know." Cyrus waved to their server.

"Oh. I didn't hear you. Lost in thought. Sorry." Amy sighed. "In any case, with people Mom knows on the verge of death, her own declining health, I'm rethinking how I approach all this traveling."

"You could always hire a couple of new photographers and let them go places."

"But what would I do then?"

"Open a studio. Teach photography. Write

books about photography. Start a family. Have kids. Take their photographs. Publish coffee table books. The list is endless."

"Did you just say kids?"

"I did? Don't remember. One more: work in Christmastown. We need all the help we can get."

"You said kids."

"I love kids." *Please let it slide.*

"So when will you have them?" Amy asked.

"I don't know. I'm too busy with Christmastown. Speaking of which, let's make a list of all the things we can do to make sure Christ has preeminence in our projects. Let's make that our Christmastown agenda."

"Seriously?"

"Isn't that what you wanted?"

"Well..."

"You said that Christmas has been too commercialized."

Amy nodded.

"So let's claim it back for Christ."

"Because Jesus is the heart of Christmas—mine, anyway."

"Mine too."

"What do you have in mind?"

"I've been mulling over this." Cyrus waved down the server to ask for more paper napkins. When the server left, he continued. "Last Christmas, Savannah and the area were overrun by Holiday Frenzy Decorators. They have the entire Santa market."

"And Christmastown banks on religious traditional themes."

Cyrus's eyes widened.

"What?" Amy asked.

"You said *banks*."

"So?"

"I thought you hated the commercialization of Christmas."

"I do..."

"But you don't want to lose the company."

"I guess not, for the sake of Grandpa Earnest's memory and my dad's legacy."

"So let me propose this," Cyrus said. "We may have to expand outside of Savannah."

"Expand? It's all going to be on you, considering I'm out of the country most of the year."

"Can you do something about that?"

"About what?"

"I don't know. You have two entirely different businesses."

"Not entirely. Photography can be seasonal."

Cyrus sat back as the server cleared the table and offered them dessert. He and Amy both declined.

*Photography can be seasonal.*

"What if you spend the Christmas season in town and stay local with your photography business?" Cyrus asked. "Then we can both run Christmastown together."

"And the rest of the year, I could go photograph weddings."

"Sounds like a plan. Surely more people marry in the warmer months."

"It's always warm somewhere, Cy...uh, Cyrus."

"You can call me Cy." Cyrus glanced at his watch. "Okay. We'd better run. The factory awaits. Let's pray about it and revisit this before you fly away again. How's that?"

Amy laughed. "Fly away again?"

"Yeah. It's like you're going out there, and we never know where you go." Cyrus picked up the tab. Signed it. "As for me, I stay put. You can always find me in the same spot, waiting for you."

# CHAPTER ELEVEN

"What's this? A conspiracy?" Amy stood rooted on the sidewalk on River Street outside Piper's Place as Cyrus held the door open for her and Mom.

She wondered how Mom and Cyrus could have plotted this unexpected meeting. In the last three days since the Macon factory visit, Amy had been busy getting up to speed with the business at Christmastown that she hadn't paid any attention to what Mom was doing.

It had been Mom's idea that they went out to dinner tonight since Amy had been at the office every day since Tuesday and not home enough.

Cyrus stood with his back against the open door. "After you, ladies."

Amy stepped aside to let some other restaurant guests enter. They looked like tourists.

"How y'all doing?" Cyrus nodded to the strangers.

Mom entered the restaurant next. She giggled and winked at Cyrus.

"I saw that!" Amy said. "I knew it. You two planned this meet-up."

"Huh?" Cyrus continued to hold the door, putting on some sort of ignorant face. "Come on, Amy. I can't hold the door forever. The AC would flow right out, and the price of our meals would go straight up."

Reluctantly, Amy walked past Cyrus. He smelled fresh. Shower fresh.

*Oh my beating heart.*

Cyrus kept up with her pace. When Amy glanced over, he had a silly grin on his face.

He pointed to his chin. "This is my signature grin."

Amy laughed so much she nearly collided with a server.

Suddenly, she came to a screeching halt, the second time this evening.

There, at the corner booth, was not only Mom, but also Jerome Pendegrast—the lifelong riverboat operator—sitting awfully close to Mom, his arm around her shoulders.

*Seriously?*

*Mr. Pendegrast! Tamsyn's dad.*

*Tamsyn from high school...*

*Her dad and my mom. That is so weird!*

Across the booth, two other people sat down quickly, chatting with Mom and Jerome like they were all old friends.

"The booth is full," Amy announced some ten feet away, standing in the middle of the restaurant surrounded by tables and people and servers and noise.

*I thought I was having dinner with Mom. Alone.*

*What to do now?*

The restaurant noise got louder around her, making it difficult to think.

She decided not to confront Mom.

She wished she had her brother Isaac's nerve to confront Mom whenever she pulled a trick like this.

But Amy wasn't Isaac.

And Isaac wasn't here to defend her or take her side now.

Besides, since Dad had passed away, Mom had been fragile. Or seemed so. Thus, whatever Rhoda Untermeyer wanted, Rhoda Untermeyer got.

When the conflicts had become too hot, too

hostile, too hard to bear, Amy and her brothers had simply left home.

They had left Mom alone to wallow in her own selfishness.

Still, Amy wondered what Mom had been doing all these years, whether she had been able to find her life after Dad—or life after the kids had grown and left the nest.

Amy had been happy to know that Mom had found a good church and that Riverside Chapel cared for its widows.

In fact, Amy liked the church herself after Mom had emailed her about it a few years back, so much so that she considered Pastor Flores her transit pastor, whose sermons she listened to in-between flights and at airport layovers all over the world.

"Super Seniors," Cyrus offered.

Amy turned. In her memory flashes, she had all but forgotten that Cyrus was nearby.

"They get together for meals, mostly brunches and dinners," he continued.

"I thought... I thought Mom and I were having dinner together. Mother-daughter activity and all that."

"Oh. I'm sorry. The Super Seniors eat here every Friday night."

"So you think..."

"Your mom forgot it's Friday. She texted me to come here so you won't have dinner alone if you didn't want to join the Super Seniors."

"She texted you?" Incredible. "When?"

"About half an hour ago."

"Just before we left the house. She didn't say anything to me in the car."

"Maybe she forgot. It can happen."

"You think her mind is going?" Amy felt alarmed. The knee replacement. The sale of Christmastown.

"I don't know, but I called ahead and got us a table."

"Cyrus, that's very kind of you, but I'm not eating dinner with you."

"We had lunch in Macon on Tuesday."

"Business lunch," Amy reminded him. She turned to leave. "I hope Jerome can give Mom a ride home—oh. We took her car."

"I'll take you home," Cyrus said.

"No need. I can call Uber." Amy walked out of Piper's Place. To her surprise, Cyrus was right behind her.

"I'll be your Uber," he said.

The air outside was cooling down in the sultry evening. It was still a little warm, but bearable with the moisture from Savannah River coming over the promenade and River Street.

Around them, pedestrians and tourists—and some rather exhausted-looking little kids in strollers—milled about. Some jaywalked among patient taxicab drivers and vehicles.

Standing on the sidewalk staring down at the cobblestone street, Amy felt a tear in her eye. Must be the dust from this old eighteenth-century town.

The dust of age and olden days and times past and lost merriment of carefree youth when nothing had mattered but the moments in front of her.

As Amy had grown up, her jaded view of life, her eroded perspectives of what once was and could never be, had all but influenced—polluted!—her worldview.

*I wish Dad were here.*

*He'd know what to do. How to handle Mom.*

"I don't like to be manipulated," Amy said quietly.

"I hear you." Cyrus dug his fingers into the pockets of his cargo shorts.

They stood facing the street.

"Has she ever done this to you?" Amy asked.

"No."

"I feel humiliated. Stood up." This was why Isaac hadn't come home in five years. Mom had pulled this sort of nonsense on them way too many times.

She would agree to something—like a sports

meet when Isaac had been on his college football team—then failed to show up when she had gotten a better offer or had found something more interesting to do, like getting a pedicure.

Mom would change her plans on a dime, often without telling anyone, but causing trouble and grief to all concerned. Like neither Isaac nor Amy —nor their other brother, Garrett—had been important enough to take first priority in Mom's life.

And now that Mom was in her seventies and perhaps needed someone to care for her, her children were nowhere to be found.

Amy had come home because she had no choice.

Perhaps it was true that selling Christmastown was the only way Mom could get her attention. But for what? Mom hadn't said much since Amy had been home five days and counting.

If not for the cancelled wedding in Kyoto, she would have been gone again for weeks, if not more.

"What's so bad about having dinner with me?" Cyrus asked. He remained beside Amy.

She glanced down to find that he was wearing boat shoes without socks. Had he hurried out of the house when Mom texted him?

"We're not having dinner together," Amy said. "This is not a blindsided date night."

"Let's take a walk then?" Cyrus smiled. "Work off our frustrations."

"Is that what you do when you're upset? Take a walk?"

"I run, actually. Or I go to the gym. Punch a few bags."

"I could use a punching bag."

"At your service, ma'am." Cyrus leaned toward her. "Just don't hit too hard."

Amy couldn't help but smile. A little, anyway.

"Look." Cyrus pointed across River Street toward the sky above Savannah River. A container ship glided by. "A flash of lightning over the island there?"

"I missed it."

"I think it's going to rain tonight. That should help your tree farm, yes?"

Amy sighed. "It's not mine. It's still in Mom's name."

"She said your dad wanted you to have it. Said that's why she couldn't sell it along with Christmastown."

"Must every discussion lead back to Mom?" Amy asked.

"You can't choose your family sometimes," Cyrus said. "Especially moms."

"Isn't that the truth!" Amy's tummy growled.

"I heard that."

"Me too. Maybe I need dinner."

"I know an ice cream place just two blocks from here," Cyrus said.

"Ice cream for dinner?"

"I had potato chips for lunch."

"That's ridiculous." Amy stepped back when a loud crowd pushed through the sidewalk.

"It was delicious. All-natural potato chips."

"I mean, don't you need to eat real meals three times a day?"

"Don't tell me what to do." Cyrus frowned. "Let me die in peace with my bag of potato chips."

*Let me die in peace.*

The same words she had encountered twice in five days. Amy's thoughts flung back to that text message she had seen on Mom's phone on Monday.

The one from a certain Walt, whom Amy might or might not know.

*No! I don't want to see her.*

*She doesn't need to know.*

*Let me die in peace.*

Who was that? Was it Uncle Walt? Was he dying of something?

*Nah.*

She shouldn't make assumptions or presume anything. There were too many Walts in the world.

But only a few Walts—maybe just one—whom Mom knew, right?

Then again, she hadn't been close to Mom in years. Other Walts could've popped up in her life.

"...watch me eat."

Cyrus was talking.

"Huh?" Amy snapped out of her stupor and suspicions.

"I need dinner," Cyrus said.

"So go eat. Don't let me stop you. Good night." Amy dug for her iPhone to call for a ride home.

"Amy."

"Yes?"

"We're here, standing in front of dozens of restaurants with open doors. Let's grab a bite, salvage our dinner. Then we can go our merry way."

Amy turned toward Cyrus. She heard laughter, looked beyond Cyrus to the crowd behind him, and that was when she saw it. In the streetlights of Savannah's River Street, the sign was visible, oddly taped over an old wrought iron tavern sign above the door of a closed shop.

*Photo Studio: For Sale*

Amy's eyes went from the sign to the windows above.

*Loft Apartment: Available*

"Seriously!" Amy blurted.

"Yeah, seriously."

Cyrus didn't seem to know what she was looking at.

"If you leave now, I'll be eating dinner alone. And so will you," he said. "At least let me buy you coffee. Kona if you want. Let me prove to you that I'm not cheap."

"Cheap?" Amy's attention swung back to Cyrus.

"You called me cheap on Monday," Cyrus reminded her.

"I did?" It felt so long ago.

"But we got along on Tuesday." Amy wasn't sure if that was enough to counter it, but she wasn't about to retract a word that could have been true on Monday.

"Yes, and the rest of the week." Cyrus's voice softened. It sounded reconciliatory. "Now it's Friday. How about we end our first working week together on a good note?"

# PART II

## LOVE

# CHAPTER TWELVE

*a*my got him thinking.

Cyrus felt like he was a stubborn guy. Sure of himself. Determined.

But Amy got him thinking that maybe his world was too small. Maybe he needed to expand his perspective. Maybe—

"Fifty-five?"

Cyrus looked up. The woman at the door was reading off a piece of paper. He raised his hand when she called his number again. He left the wall he had been leaning on while waiting in the passport line at the post office. He handed her his paperwork as he stepped into the office and into a new world.

*For me.*

"Looks like you need photos taken."

"Yes, ma'am."

She told him the cost. Told him where to stand.

He stood there to get his mug shot.

She told him he had to turn his face this way, tilt his chin that way.

Snap. Snap.

The camera flash made Cyrus think of Amy Untermeyer, professional photographer. He doubted if he could ever look at another camera without thinking of Amy.

A woman of mystery—somewhat.

Even after Mrs. Untermeyer had told him a lot about Amy's childhood, there were still many frames missing from her life that he hadn't been privy to. Those years she had traveled the world after college to pursue a photography career.

Where was she was in Hawaii?

Cyrus wished he were with her. Of all the people in the world, he had finally found someone he wanted to be with.

Maybe for the rest of his life.

"Please have a seat."

Cyrus did what he was told. He sat there quietly, as if waiting for a verdict. The lady behind the desk looked at his paperwork, which he had filled out by hand. Printed his letters as nicely as he could, as if he were going to get a school grade for it.

"Going anywhere soon?"

Cyrus wondered if it was standard to be asked about his travel plans. "Maybe. My girl—uh, someone I like—travels a lot, and I'm thinking I'm missing out on something if I don't have a passport."

"Where is she now?"

"Hawaii." As he said the word, Cyrus began to miss Amy.

The clerk laughed. "You don't need a passport to go to Hawaii, you know. It's the fiftieth state of the union."

"I know." His face reddened. "You asked me."

"Well, I'm asking if you're going anywhere soon because if you are, I would suggest expediting the passport—it would cost more—but if you have time, then we'll do the usual route."

"Which would be?" Cyrus asked, calming down.

"About four to six weeks."

"And if I want it fast?"

"We can do it in a couple of weeks, or same day if you're in an emergency."

"No emergency." *Thank God.*

The nice lady told Cyrus how much he had to pay in total. She swiped his credit card and sent him out the door.

Six weeks.

Cyrus stepped into the August rain. It was warm.

And he wanted to share it with Amy.

*What in the world?*

He made a dash for Uncle Mel's car and hopped in, his wet shirt sticking to his shoulders.

Did rain feel the same way in Hawaii—where Amy was—or in Alaska—where she would be next?

As he drove back to the Christmastown warehouse, Cyrus wondered what it would be like to get on an airplane and be lifted up in the air—

*Yikes.*

Thirty thousand feet in the air?

He looked through the windshield, through the dissipating rain, and up into the dark clouds.

*No, thanks.*

*I'll stick to cars and trains.*

But.

There was Amy.

He had just sent off his passport application.

*Okay. I can do this.*

*Baby steps. Baby steps.*

# CHAPTER THIRTEEN

o, it wasn't a good idea to cater to the last-minute whims of a tipsy bride-to-be who decided that she wanted to get her photographs taken in her grandfather's pineapple plantation, wearing her expensive and delicate lace wedding gown.

Amy's photography crew followed the woman all over the fields, watching her wedding gown being ripped to shreds by the razor-sharp pineapple leaves.

Almost five hundred snapshots later, Amy and her crew returned to their beachfront hotel in Oahu, covered with cuts and scrapes all over their arms and exposed thighs and calves.

Amy took a long, hot shower, washed her hair, applied some antiseptic to her cuts, and then sat down to check her emails. It was a good thing she was decently dressed, because Cyrus wanted to chat.

"Yikes. Hope those cuts don't get infected," he said over Skype.

Amy retracted her waving arms from her laptop camera. "We're back on Oahu, and the wedding coordinator is scrambling to find a replacement gown before the sunrise wedding."

"See what I mean? Those destination weddings are a lot of hassle."

"Maybe. It can also bring many happy memories."

"I prefer to see happy memories in the marriage."

"Ah, ever the practical man, you are," Amy said.

Of course, she had only known Cyrus for mere weeks and couldn't begin to know how practical he really was. However, from what she had seen so far, he was down to earth. And as practical as they came.

Except for that Friday night dinner on Jekyll Island when Cyrus had spent an untold amount to take her out to dinner just to prove that he wasn't cheap. They had driven an hour south to Saffron on Jekyll, a Michelin-rated restaurant Amy had never heard of.

Since it had been a warm night, the maître d'hôtel had not insisted that Cyrus wear a jacket. With Cyrus wearing a tee shirt and faded cargo shorts, and Amy wearing a simple summer dress, they showed up, famished, at their call-ahead rooftop table.

Amy had a wonderful evening. It was not only some of the best dishes she had tasted, but Cyrus was funny in his own way, cracking jokes about Uncle Mel's antics when he had been younger.

"I can't believe it's been three weeks since I left Savannah," Amy said into the camera.

"Please don't tell me you don't trust my running Christmastown."

"It's only August, Cyrus. The jury is still out until December."

"Oh, the pressure."

"Don't fail the Untermeyer family now."

"I'll try not to." Cyrus munched on something.

"What is that?"

"Uh, just some cookies your mom made."

When Amy opened her mouth to ask for more information—like, what sort of cookies?—Cyrus lifted his hand to stop her. "Come home and get some yourself."

*Come home?*

Was Savannah home to her? She wasn't sure.

# CHAPTER FOURTEEN

"*H*ow's the pop-up tree coming along?" Amy asked. "Did they fix the problem?"

Cyrus swallowed the last bit of cookie before he answered Amy's question. They had developed a business rapport, come to an understanding, and he didn't want to lose whatever bits—or wisps—of harmony between them.

Right now, Amy seemed to be comfortable talking with him on video. Her hair was wrapped up in a hotel towel, and she was smiling, in spite of those scratches from the pineapple plantation. Perhaps it was the distance between them or the natural divide that was in virtual environments.

Cyrus was more of a people person. He'd rather talk to people face to face, but the internet had afforded him somewhat of a safe zone—so to speak—to interact with Amy. Perhaps if they got to know each other more, they could truly become a team and run Christmastown like Mrs. U had done with her husband.

That husband-and-wife team had been successful for decades until Mr. U had passed away.

*Husband-and-wife team?*

Cyrus began to choke.

"Hey, you okay there?" Amy asked.

Cyrus held up a finger as he downed half a bottle of Gatorade. His windpipe cleared. "What was your question again?"

"Is your pop-up Christmas tree popping up?" Amy smiled.

Cyrus barely nodded. "Well, Fred at the factory said his engineers need a couple more months."

"So we're looking at September? October? Will we have enough time to distribute it?"

*We?*

*Did she just say we?*

Cyrus began to think that his prayers were being answered. Yes, he wanted so badly to work together with Amy. He'd rather have peace with her at forty-nine percent of the company than buy her out. It was more fun to have someone else partnering with him than to go solo.

Funny how his view of businesses sort of mirrored his personal life. He'd been single for a long time. It seemed that there came a time when he would like to find a wife and settle down. Do things together with her, raise kids with her, and...

He gulped.

*Maybe even go places with her...*

For that, he'd need a passport.

"Earth to Cyrus. Come in, Cyrus?" Amy laughed.

"Sorry. Chasing rabbits."

"I figured. Maybe you should go to bed. It's late over there. I have to get up early and go to work."

"Yes, a wedding to shoot." Cyrus nodded. "I'm glad you're doing well and survived today."

"Let me know when Fred fixes the tree."

"His engineers and I have discussed it. The prototype works."

Amy nodded. "We just need to pray for God's will to be done here."

"And if it's not God's will for us to sell this tree, then so be it."

"Yeah. We still have that tree farm."

"*You* have it, not me. It's not a Christmastown business." *Not yet.*

"Do you want it to be?"

"I won't hide the fact that, yes, I think it should be part of Christmastown, but if we bring it in, you will then have a majority share of the company."

"And that scares you?" Amy asked.

Cyrus couldn't read her face on screen, not with the towel wrapped around her head. The only thing he could see was that she was losing her smile. Perhaps she was tired from a long day, but perhaps their relationship still needed work. It could be tenuous at times, and any slight misstep on his part could ruin it for them.

Or not?

"Scared? Maybe just a little bit," Cyrus confessed.

"Well, Cyrus, how about trusting God to make our paths smooth? Is He not the God of peace?"

"Yes, He is."

After he said a reluctant goodbye to Amy, Cyrus began to pray in his heart.

*Lord Jesus, please have Your way in Christmastown. I surrender the company to You to do as You please.*

Cyrus felt a heavy burden lifted off his chest.

It was freeing to seek the Lord and place his livelihood at the foot of the cross of Christ.

*I carry the burden no more, for my God carries it for me. He is able. Way more than able.*

# CHAPTER FIFTEEN

*A*my had four days to catch up with Cyrus and the happenings at Christmastown.

Then it was off to Alaska to snap the memories of someone else's family reunion in Anchorage, and to the Denali National Park for a bridal magazine photo shoot. It was the end of summer, and the fireweeds were having their last hurrah with their bright magenta petals.

But first, Christmastown.

Even though it was only August, the Christmas buzz was beginning to build.

Cyrus was in his office interviewing potential seasonal workers, and the applications had started to pile up.

Rasheed Bolton was showing her his new

RFID software to track down every piece of inventory in the entire building.

"Down to the last mini ornament," he said. "And you know how tiny that can get."

"I'm impressed." Amy shook her head as he pointed here and there on the large touch-screen monitor.

There were several workstations around the warehouse connected to the database via land lines, but mostly, Amy knew the warehouse workers all had Wi-Fi tablets.

"The cost savings are tremendous. In the last year alone, we shaved off forty percent of waste."

"Wow. Good job."

"Well, we prayed and asked the Lord for wisdom, and He gives beyond measure."

"That's the truth. Way beyond measure." Amy was still staring at the screen. "Now show me the customer-management system. Can we meet demands this year?"

"That's what we've been upgrading all summer, ma'am. Hard to compete with Holiday Frenzy."

Amy nodded. "Progress report?"

"We've been testing, and I think we're almost there."

"When do you go live?"

"I hope next week."

End of August. "Just in time to catch the reservations and orders in September."

"Pray it will all work out."

"I will. I'm glad you're a praying man too, Rasheed. We need God's anointing in this place so we don't lose our focus on what matters."

Rasheed nodded. "I'm praying for you and Cyrus."

"Thank you. Exactly what are you praying for?" Amy was curious now.

A deacon from Riverside Chapel praying for her and Cyrus? Why?

"That you two will get enough rest. Both of you work very hard, I'm gathering."

"Yeah. I need a long sabbatical. All that traveling is wrecking my body."

"I believe you. When I take the family to see their grandparents in Arizona, it wears me out. Plain wears me out. My wife too. She said we should fly. But when you have six kids..."

"I hear you."

"So we take the family van and tough it out."

*Tough it out.*

"That's what I do. Tough it out," Amy said. "Rasheed?"

"Yes, ma'am?"

"If you're praying for me, please pray for God's

will in my life. I want His perfect will more than anything else in the world."

"That's a great desire." Rasheed nodded, like he was filing it away in his mind. "I'm sure God will honor that."

"I've come to this point in my life where I've done what I wanted—be the best professional photographer I can be. But it's draining me." Amy sighed. "I love the job, the income, the travels, but I'm going to be thirty soon, and I can't imagine living out of a suitcase the rest of my career, you know. I don't even own my own home... Why am I telling you all this?"

"Because I'm a deacon at your church—the one you visit, anyway—and you know I will not pray against God."

Amy nodded.

"I know what you're saying," Rasheed said. "You need an anchor. And of course, you know that your anchor is Jesus Christ."

Amy nodded again.

"Each of us has a calling. You want to know what—and where—God is calling you."

"Thank you, Rasheed."

"I'm praying for God's will for Cyrus's life also."

"That's always the right prayer," Amy

concluded just as someone crossed the floor toward them.

"Miss Untermeyer?" she said.

"Amy."

"Miss Amy, there's someone here to see you. Said you don't know her, but her name is Meadow Lark Oberon-Greene."

"Seriously?" Amy chuckled. "Is that even a real name? Meadow Lark—"

*Oberon.*

Amy hadn't heard that name in a very long time, not since she was six years old.

It was Uncle Walt's last name.

Walter Oberon.

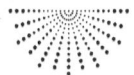

# CHAPTER SIXTEEN

"*Y*ou lied to me!" Amy shouted the moment she spotted Mom among the Christmas trees, some of which were taller than she was.

Apparently Mom hadn't heard her, as she continued to move among the trees.

It was a good thing too, because Mom was surrounded by people Amy didn't know, except for Jerome Pendegrast, who seemed to be walking too closely to Mom. Hovering?

Amy drew a deep breath.

Blinked away a tear.

*Lord Jesus, I can't do this.*

She turned to get back to her car, but someone called her name.

"My daughter is here!"

Mom's voice.

*How could she sound so happy?*

Amy steeled herself. Clenched her fists.

*Lord Jesus, please give me grace.*

"Come meet my one and only daughter." Mom made a beeline toward Amy, and the rest of her group followed. "Friends, this is Amy Untermeyer."

"Ah, Amy's Christmas Tree Farm. That makes sense," someone said.

"Amy is almost twenty-eight—she was a December baby—and she's single and eligible, if any of your grandsons are looking for the perfect girlfriend."

"Mom!" Amy couldn't believe Mom had said that.

Everyone chuckled or giggled or made strange noises. Then they started chatting among themselves. Amy heard male names rising in the cacophony.

Jerome cleared his throat. "Folks, are we going to finish the tour or not? We have reservations for lunch at my riverboat, and if we miss it, there's no refund!"

He ushered Mom away.

She turned her head. "I'll see you at home, dear, unless you want to join us for lunch? I'm sure we can always add a ticket."

"Oh no, thanks. You go ahead. I'll talk with you at home."

Mom furrowed her brows. "I'll be home by two or three, unless we decide to go shopping—again. I'll text you."

"You do that." Amy waved feebly as she was left standing alone among a cluster of dwarf spruce trees, all in silent rows, all pointing toward the sky.

The midmorning sky outside Savannah was cloudy and dark. Like it was going to rain something fierce.

Amy stared up as tears flowed down her cheeks.

*Lord Jesus, what do I do now?*

# CHAPTER SEVENTEEN

*I*t would be more than five hours later before Mom came home from her Super Seniors shopping trip. Jerome Pendegrast stuck to her like glue and made coffee in Mom's kitchen.

Amy endured another thirty minutes of drinking coffee in silence before Jerome left the house.

In retrospect, she could have gone to her room to weep or sulk or something. But she didn't want Mom to somehow leave with Jerome or do something else that would cause Amy to wait longer for this talk.

After Mom and Amy had put away the saucers in the dishwasher, Mom wiped the countertop where Jerome had spilled water in his effort to make coffee and impress his girlfriend.

Mom said nothing.

Amy wondered if Mom had forgotten that they had something to discuss, or whether she hoped that by keeping quiet, they didn't have to talk about what was on Amy's mind.

But.

It was time.

"Mom?" Amy asked as Mom wrung out the dishcloth and placed it at the edge of the sink as she had always done.

"Yes?" Mom sat down at the breakfast nook.

Amy leaned against the kitchen island.

"It's about Jerome, isn't it?" Mom asked in a low voice. "You don't approve."

"Huh? No—I mean, not—I mean, I don't care about Jerome."

"You don't care?" Mom asked, pain in her face.

"Well, not like that. Jerome is the least of my worries."

Mom's left hand went up to her chest, and there it was.

Amy saw the diamond.

On. Her. Ring. Finger.

"You're getting remarried?" Amy asked, holding on to the granite countertop behind her.

"He asked me this morning." Mom smiled, but

her eyes were staring straight at Amy. "We went to the jewelry store after lunch so I could pick my own diamond. Do you think your dad would mind my remarrying?"

"Dad?" Amy's knees went weak. *Which one?*

"Yes, your dad. I've always loved only him."

"Dad?"

"Yes, and I wish he never died in that car wreck. It was so terrible." Mom wiped tears from her eyes. Reached for a paper napkin at the edge of the small table. "I've never been the same since."

"Dad." *Felix Untermeyer. The only dad I ever knew.*

*Dad, I miss you so much!*

"I miss your dad." Mom slid the engagement ring off her finger. "I'll have to tell Jerome I can't go through with it."

*What do I tell her?*

"Mom, in God's plan for families on earth, marriages last only until we die. There are no marriages in heaven."

Mom nodded.

"When Dad passed away, your marriage was over. You were free to marry again."

"I didn't want to. Still don't."

"Have you prayed about it before you said yes or no to Jerome?"

"No. He caught me by surprise. He spent a

pretty penny on that ring." She stared at that white-gold ring with a cluster of diamonds on the table.

"I must say that's a pretty ring," Amy said. "How long have you been an item?"

"A couple of years since Super Seniors became an active group..."

It seemed to Amy that Mom had more to say.

"But your dad can never be replaced." She dabbed her eyes.

"No. Never. But life goes on, right?" Amy wasn't sure she believed that herself. Did life really go on? Things had not been the same since Dad had been gone. Still, how could one keep on grieving some seven or eight years later?

"Jerome's wife passed away years ago also. He never forgot her."

"We'll always remember our loved ones."

Mom nodded. Blew her nose.

"So how about if you pray about it and see what God says?" Amy said softly, all her anger disappearing into the air—or was being tucked away for now. How could she be upset with Mom in her present state? "Don't make decisions based on knee-jerk reactions."

*Whoa. Is that a note to myself?*

*Have I been reacting to this entire Uncle Walt situation impetuously?*

"Would you pray for me?" Mom asked.

"Yes, Mom. I will. Let's pray now." Amy sat down across from Mom and held her trembling, fragile hands in hers. "Nothing God can't handle."

*Yep. Nothing God can't handle.*

# CHAPTER EIGHTEEN

*W*ithin twenty-four hours, Amy had flown out of Savannah, one week too early and twenty-eight years too late, her breakfast conversation with Mom still fresh in her mind.

She had told Mom over two scrambled eggs and toast that she would be back soon and they needed to talk about something very important.

"What about?" Mom asked as she buttered her toast.

"I'd rather not talk about it now. We're eating. Don't want to spoil our appetite."

Mom's toast slipped from her fingers. "You're pregnant."

Amy didn't know whether to laugh or cry over Mom's cluelessness.

"No, I'm not."

"Oh good. I want you to find the perfect man." Mom picked up her toast.

"There is no such thing as a perfect man, according to Dad."

"He's right—was right." Mom munched on toast.

Amy watched her eat.

Waited.

Mom ate very slowly, as if buying time.

In a way, Amy didn't want to bring it up. Not this early in the morning, though it was almost eight. She had planned on going to the Christmas-town warehouse—that also housed its headquarters —to see what was required of her as the vice president.

"So. What is the taboo topic?" Mom asked.

"It's not taboo. Just some new development in our family." Amy drank her orange juice. It had pulp in it, but it was too sweet for her, regardless. She went to the refrigerator and found a bottled water. "Want some?"

"No." Mom lifted her steamy cup of coffee.

Amy slid back onto the bench.

"New development in our family, you say?" Mom said. "You don't like Jerome?"

Amy knew she couldn't hold it off any longer. If she left town without clearing the air with Mom, she knew that Mom would spend the next however many days coming up with theories and suspicions. Her imagination could run amuck sometimes.

"All right. I wasn't going to talk about it now, but seeing that you're almost done with breakfast..."

"Go on." Mom drank coffee. She had that worried look on her forehead.

The same kind of worried look Amy had known all her life. The one before the storm came, before the impending grounding. The same look she'd had when Amy's and her brothers' school teachers handed them a D or an F on their chapter tests.

"Explain Uncle Walt," Amy said.

"That's easy. His kidneys don't work anymore."

"And?"

Slowly, Mom spoke. "I see. You're wondering about the text message he sent me a month ago. He's dying."

"And?"

"I told him you should know because he had been a big part of your life until you were about six years old, always bringing you presents."

"Cheap presents that broke on the first day we played with them?"

"It's the thought that counts."

"That's what they all said."

Silence between them was marred by the

outdoor sounds of dogs barking and a lawn mower spluttering next door.

"And?" Amy tried again.

"I have to abide by his wishes."

"And continue to live the lie?" Amy pushed. She watched Mom's face change.

"I don't know what happened..." Mom's shoulders slacked. "It was so long ago, though."

"Still in my lifetime."

"I loved your dad very much."

"Sure. Did he know?"

Mom nodded. "It was a mistake. A big mistake."

"I'm a mistake." Amy's heart broke.

"No, Amy. No. You were never—no. I wanted you. Your dad wanted you. He didn't want a divorce."

Amy leaned back against the bench. The padding was still cushiony against her shoulder blades. "You cheated on Dad."

"He wanted a daughter."

"Aarrgh! That makes no sense," Amy said. "Dad wanted a daughter, so you gave him one?"

"He wanted you afterwards."

It seemed to Amy that the more Mom tried to explain, the worse it got. Eventually the truth had to be told, but Amy knew she could no longer be in the same house as Mom. In this very house she had grown up in with parents who had kept such a dark secret from her.

"What about Garrett? Is he Dad's?" Amy had to know. Garrett had brown hair, like Dad used to before it had all fallen out.

Mom nodded. There was no hesitation there.

"So... Garrett is Dad's only child. Isaac was adopted when he was four. And I'm the product of an affair. Some happy family we have."

"To be fair, your dad and I weren't getting along for a spell."

"Fair to whom, Mom?" Amy caught herself. Regardless of what Mom had done—or hadn't done—she would always still be Mom. "There's no excuse, right? For better, for worse, right? You broke your marriage vows."

"And your dad forgave me."

That would be how Dad was. Always forgiving. Always giving people second chances.

Amy remembered how Dad had recited Scripture passages on forgiveness. She hadn't known why he had insisted that she memorize those verses in high school and beyond.

Now it was all clear.

Dad had known that someday, she was going to need those verses, verses like Ephesians 4:32.

Amy closed her eyes. She could see Dad

walking with her through the Christmas tree farm and talking with her.

"Be kind to your mother, Amy. She has had a hard life. 'And be ye kind one to another, tender-hearted, forgiving one another, even as God for Christ's sake hath forgiven you.'"

*Be kind to your mother.*

Even then, Dad had prepared her. That had been four or five years before that fatal wreck in the middle of the highway. The horrible visit by two police officers hours later, bearing the bad news that had torn the family apart.

*Dad, I miss you so much!*

*And you're my only dad. Forever.*

"When did Dad find out?" Amy's voice cracked.

"When you were six."

*Woe is me.*

"You kept the secret from Dad for six years?" *And from me for twenty-eight years—well, twenty-seven plus nine months.*

"He was busy with Christmastown night and day, year in, year out."

"Only from September to December. I was born in December."

Mom shrugged.

Amy didn't prod any further. There was no

need. She had been conceived in March when it was off season for the family business. At least Mom hadn't played around during one of the most sacred times of the year. How horrible it would've been had Amy been born in, say September, or thereabouts.

The dalliance—the extramarital sin!—had been committed in March... But how long had it gone on?

"How long, Mom?"

"It just happened, then it was over."

"Nothing *just* happened. Was Uncle Walt coming on to you?"

"He always came on to the ladies."

"I wouldn't call them *ladies* if they were sleeping around."

Mom sprang up from her seat. The coffee mug tipped over, spilling last bits of coffee onto the table. She left it that way and strutted out of the kitchen.

It was then that Amy realized she walked like Mom.

Amy cleaned up the spill, loaded and started the dishwasher, and went upstairs to her room to pack. She had been living out of her suitcase, and packing only meant grabbing her toothbrush, tooth-paste, and toiletries from the bathroom and stuffing them back into her rolling carryon.

Rescheduling her flight took more than half an hour, but once done, it was done.

She left a note on the kitchen table and drove to the airport.

Two hours later, she was at her gate at the Savannah / Hilton Head International Airport.

Seven hours after the airplane took off, she was in her window seat getting a bird's-eye view of the Seattle/Tacoma International Airport.

Five hours after she picked up her rental SUV, she arrived at a resort hotel room on Cannon Beach in Oregon in the middle of the night.

Alone where no one knew her, she wept her eyes out.

# CHAPTER NINETEEN

"God made you, little sister, no matter who your parents are." Isaac's voice was steady and calm on the phone, but he sounded like he wanted to punch something.

He also sounded tired, and Amy didn't want to keep him up too long. It was past eleven at night in Sydney, where his cruise ship was docked for the night. He had called her after she had sent him a long email about the news.

As Amy listened to her brother speak encouraging words to her—as he had always done—she relaxed on the chaise lounge on the covered deck of her top-floor hotel room.

It was after seven in the morning, and the sun had risen in the sky, coming up behind the resort and heading for the Pacific Ocean.

In the distance, she could see bits of the top of Ecola State Park and Chapman Point to her right, and Haystack Rock to her left.

In front of her was the vast expanse of Cannon Beach, the Pacific Ocean that stretched all the way to Hawaii and Japan, and the big old sky that almighty God had made.

All a reminder that life went on. God's sunrise and sunset continued on.

She could spend days and evenings here, photographing.

And that was what she had intended to do until it was time to drive back to Seattle to fly to Alaska to the next project.

For now, she had to process her life-changing news alone—yet not so alone. She had called Isaac, knowing her brother would help her through this mess.

*God made you, little sister, no matter who your parents are.*

"Is that what you told yourself when you were shuttled from foster home to foster home?" Amy asked.

"No. I was too young to notice. As long as someone changed my diapers, I don't think I cared." Isaac chuckled.

"Dad always said that when he saw you, he knew you were going to be his son."

"Yes." Isaac went silent for a bit on the phone. Then he cleared his throat. "He will always be my dad."

"Mine too. No matter what."

"You have your own life now, and I'm glad you're doing well," Isaac said.

"How can I go back to Savannah ever again?"

"For Dad's memories, someday I will go back to Savannah."

Somehow, Amy knew he would. "We have stayed away because Mom is difficult to live with."

"Even Garrett."

"But you know what I found out?" Amy asked.

"What? Garrett's adopted too?"

"No. He's flesh and blood. What I found out is that Mom is a mixed bag. She has helped a lot of people at church. And yet she has also been very needy. Some people like her because she'd babysit anyone's kids, sometimes without pay if they couldn't afford it. And at other times, she calls the church office to talk to the pastor umpteen times a day about all sorts of issues and ailments and whatnots."

"Sounds like she has two personalities?"

"No. Sounds like someone had better keep an eye on her now that she's in her seventies." Amy couldn't believe she even said that, let alone imply that one of them—estranged as they were—would have to take care of Mom in Savannah.

"Yes. You can't see me, but I'm nodding in agreement."

"Okay."

"I wish I could go home to Savannah with you, Amy."

Amy sat up. "You said home."

"What?"

"You said go *home* to Savannah, not *visit* Savannah."

"I guess I did."

Amy closed her eyes. "Savannah will always be home to us, right?"

"I can't go home right away though. My contract is for another year. Since we're cruising around the world, I can't just jump off the ship whenever I want, you know."

"So when do you have any time off?"

"It used to be in the winter, when the coastal areas are somewhat frozen, but this cruise is in the Southern Hemisphere where it's summer in December."

"Right."

"So the next time I get a break, it'll probably be May or June or later."

"It'll be here before we know it," Amy decided.

"You get to try my new dish."

"Yeah?"

"I named it after you," Isaac said.

"Seriously? Not one of your bitter melon concoctions, I hope. It'd better be sweet."

"Oh it is, but not as sweet as you."

"Sure." Amy stepped back into her hotel room and closed the sliding glass door.

It was almost time to shower and then go wander around the area to take random photos. It would be a far cry from the scheduled photo shoots and choreographed wedding photos or events.

*Just point and shoot whatever shows up.*

"Well, little sister, I have to run," Isaac said. "It's almost one in the morning here."

"Sorry to keep you up." Really. She hadn't emailed Isaac to have him call her instead of sending his usual short replies days later.

"No, I'm glad we talked. What time is it over there?"

"Almost eight."

"What are you going to do today?" Isaac had often wanted to know such things about Amy.

"Take random photos all day long, eat food, gripe, and try to recover from the mess that is our family."

Isaac chuckled. "Wish I could be lazy like that. Eat, sleep, rot away the hours."

"Well, you have to save up to buy a restaurant. Any closer to that?"

"Almost there."

Amy decided that if she had any extra money, she would help Isaac. It had been his lifelong dream—since high school—to run his own restaurant. He had gone to cooking school to be a chef, and he had worked very hard to rise to the rank of chef de cuisine, but to own a restaurant? That seemed to be years away.

"For the record, I'm not rotting away the hours. I'm going to test out a new Canon lens I bought," Amy justified.

"Really? How many Canons and Nikons do you have?"

"That's beside the point."

Isaac laughed loudly. "Well, I'll let you go waste your day. I miss you, little sister."

"I miss you too, big brother."

"See what I mean?" Isaac said. "God made us a family."

Yes, indeed.

*God made us a family.*

# CHAPTER TWENTY

The cliffs of Ecola State Park jutted into the Pacific Ocean in such a precarious way that Amy often thought that an accident was about to happen whenever she walked along the edges of the grass, looking for the perfect spot to catch the setting sun on Cannon Beach below and beyond.

There were people on the sandy shores—which she could Photoshop out later, if she wanted—but she was here precisely for that: impromptu life pictures.

The late afternoon wind picked up a bit, loosening strands of her hair. In one quick, experienced move, the wind slapped off her baseball cap. She let it go, as she could always get another cap.

Her new lens, however, had cost a fortune, and

she had to make sure her camera equipment didn't tip over the tripod she had tried to anchor to the soil.

She stood there waiting.

Waiting.

Looking into her lens, it blurred, and then something came into focus—

A face.

She grunted. A tourist standing in front of her camera? *Say it isn't so.*

She straightened up—

"Cyrus!"

The tripod nearly lost its balance. Amy grabbed it quickly with one hand, the other hand still on her camera, and both of her eyes on Cyrus Theroux.

Her jaw dropped.

"I'm really here," Cyrus declared.

"Keep stepping backwards and you'll be really dead."

"What?" Cyrus turned to look, and yowled. He lurched forward, away from the eroding soil.

"What are you doing here?" Amy asked.

"To see you." Cyrus walked past Amy.

Her eyes followed him. He went to a medium-sized brown box he had apparently left on the ground somewhere behind Amy.

"Oh dear. Is that what I think it is?" Amy asked.

Cyrus brought the box toward her. "Merry early Christmas."

"Is it finally working?"

"Shall we see?"

"You haven't tested it?"

"Well, yes, but that was a ton of hours ago back in Savannah."

"You drove here?" Amy raised her eyebrows.

"Not enough time."

The realization half-amused Amy. "Did you get sick onboard?"

"My doc gave me some airsick meds. Slept like a baby through the flight."

"Good for you. And who's handling the company while you're here?"

"Rasheed." Cyrus didn't look too happy.

"Then why the frown? Rasheed can run the company without us."

"I know."

Amy figured he would have to work out that issue for himself. "How long are you here?"

"Just until tomorrow afternoon. Is there a church we can attend in the morning?"

Amy nodded. She wasn't sure what to make of this visit. "You're really here to see me?"

"I want to bring you a pop-up Christmas tree

that works, and I want to see for myself that you're okay." Cyrus stepped closer to Amy.

Amy waited.

*He has overcome his fear of flying to be with me.*

The fact was not lost on her.

Cyrus reached for her hand. Touched her fingers.

She didn't pull away. Instead, she locked her fingers in his.

"Where will you be next week?" Cyrus asked.

"Alaska for the next three weeks. Then it depends on whether Midori—one of my photographers—is swamped. We fill in for one another if needed." Amy sighed. "I could use a better assistant."

"Well, your assistant—Daisy, right?—was the one who told me where to find you."

"So she did something right?"

"Don't be too hard on her. Have you ever considered that maybe you're overscheduled to begin with, and your crew, team, and employees are all scrambling to make it happen for you?"

Amy considered that a moment. "Maybe I need a better scheduling software and statistical analysis to see where we've overbooked and under-booked and see how to fix that and become more efficient?"

"Uh-huh. And I can help you with that,

considering Rasheed and I reorganized Christmas-town to make it leaner. Did you know we saved another twenty percent off expenses?"

"That's great, Cy. How much would this business consultation cost?"

"Only a date night."

"You want dinner out in exchange for helping me organize my photography business?"

"I'd even pay for dinner. You part is to show up."

Amy shuddered. "If you want dinner in Savannah, I don't know when I'll be back there. I can't—I just can't..."

Cyrus drew her to his chest. "Shhh. It's going to be okay."

"You heard?"

"Yes."

"The whole church?"

"No. Just me. When you left town abruptly on Wednesday, it didn't make sense. I was sure it was related to that visitor you had at the warehouse on Tuesday."

"Yeah."

"So I called your mom, and we had a chat." Cyrus hugged Amy tightly. "I'm here for you, whatever you need. With God's help, all will be well."

Amy nodded into his chest.

"If you must know, your mom is suffering too," Cyrus added.

"Sure."

"Seriously. She was in the hospital yesterday for exhaustion."

"What?"

"Don't worry. Jerome's right there by her side, taking care of her. They're considering moving to the Savannah Senior Living Resort on Tybee Island. Jerome's moving out of his riverboat, and your mom is selling her house."

"She can't sell our family home."

"She told me there were too many unhappy memories there."

Amy gasped. Closed her eyes. Shame overcame her. "Dad loved that house. He built it."

"I'm sorry. I didn't mean to be the bearer of bad news," Cyrus said. "Let's talk about happy things."

"Like your pop-up Christmas tree?"

Cyrus nodded.

"I don't want to open it here. Let's take it back to the hotel. Where are you staying tonight?"

"At the same hotel you're in."

"Daisy."

"She's quite efficient if you don't work her to death," Cyrus teased.

Before Amy could defend herself, Cyrus's thumb and finger were caressing her chin.

She closed her eyes as his warm lips met hers oh so gently, as if he was afraid that if he kissed her roughly, she would back away, out of his life.

Instead, she stepped forward so he could deepen the kiss.

At that precise moment, a quietude overcame Amy. She suspected that Cyrus felt it too. She heard his steady heartbeat amid the calming winds and people walking around them in the small state park.

They surfaced for air soon enough to catch the last glimpse of the sunset over the Pacific Ocean.

As Amy leaned against Cyrus's sturdy chest, Cyrus wrapped his arms around Amy, his chin resting on her shoulder.

For the first time in many years, Amy stared—not through her camera, but with her own bare eyes—at the glorious orange and yellow colors merging with pink cirrus clouds and purple strokes of beauty glowing in the western sky, reflecting off the ocean surface, a picturesque beauty that could only be photographed into her mind.

Imprinted into Amy's memory was yet another example of God's handiwork on the universe, a reminder of His glorious creation.

In Amy's heart, she felt awe.

Only awe.

# CHAPTER TWENTY-ONE

*T*hey arrived at the hotel at the same time, parked next to each other, and entered the lobby together. It wasn't appropriate for Cyrus or Amy to go to each other's hotel room, so Cyrus suggested they test out the Christmas tree in one of the empty meeting or conference rooms.

"I don't think anyone would mind," Cyrus said.

Unfortunately, the rooms were booked, and they ended up in the continental breakfast nook, which was empty at dusk.

"Ready?" Cyrus asked.

Amy nodded.

Cyrus pushed the box to the center of the nook.

"I present to you your very own pop-up

Christmas tree." Cyrus made some motion and sound.

Across the hallway, the receptionists looked up.

Some hotel guests stopped walking, as if the town crier had spoken.

Cyrus peeled back the top of the box and pulled out what looked like an egg-shaped earth tone pod or giant seed. He placed it on the carpet floor. He unlatched the side of the pod. Inside was a pile of green plastic that would pass off as leaves.

Reaching into his jean pocket, he found his remote.

"Is that what I think it is?" Amy asked.

"Yes. As soon as you mentioned it, I asked Fred to make it happen."

"And so he did. Now let's see if the remote works."

"You want to push the button?" Cyrus offered her the remote.

"Well..."

A boy tugged at Cyrus's plaid shirt. "May I push the button?"

Standing next to the boy, his mother nodded. "He loves buttons. And he loves Christmas."

"I do too." Cyrus handed the boy the remote.

As soon as he pushed the left button, the bundle of fake leaves shook and rattled.

The boy squealed in delight as the Christmas tree shot out of the pod and opened up like a noisy automatic umbrella. The tree was no more than four feet tall.

Everyone clapped.

Cyrus asked the boy to push the right button.

Lights flashed on all around the tree. Blinking. Chasing.

More applause.

"It comes in three sizes, ladies and gentlemen." Cyrus felt like a ringmaster. "Two, four, and six feet."

"Well?" Cyrus trained his eyes on Amy's. He wanted to know what his partner—business partner!—thought. "You like?"

"I love it!" Amy seemed impressed. "Wow."

Cyrus beamed with delight. "The lady approves!"

Everyone clapped again.

Somewhere in the crowd, a man in a tie stepped forward. "Question?"

"Yes, sir?"

"Where did you buy the tree?"

"Our company, Christmastown, produces it. I brought it to show Amy here that it works."

"Well, I own a chain of resorts, and I would like to place an order for a few hundred of these. When do you ship them out?"

"We've been taking orders for September through November." Cyrus logged in to the Wi-Fi network in the hotel, accessed Rasheed's super-duper ordering system, and helped the man place his order for three hundred six-foot pop-up Christmas trees to be delivered in late September.

He exchanged phone numbers with the man and then turned around to find Amy missing.

Before he could go look for her, a woman asked him if he had a Victorian pop-up tree.

"Ma'am, if you go to our Christmastown website, there's a section for custom pop-up trees, and you can select your choices," Cyrus said. "In fact, you can also have different thematic trees for every room in the house."

"That would be lovely. The kids would love to have their own Christmas trees."

"Ornaments are not included," Cyrus added. "Neither is the battery, but it does come with a power cord."

Cyrus spotted Amy coming out of the ladies' room. Was it the poor lighting, or was Amy's nose red?

He handed his business card to the couple. "The website address is on the back of the card. Check out the options and customize your pop-up Christmas trees. The sooner you do, the sooner they will be delivered. Christmastown gets super busy between the months of October and December."

He bid a quick goodbye and left his demo tree in the nook while he chased after Amy.

# CHAPTER TWENTY-TWO

*U*ncle Walt lived with his daughter, Meadow Lark Oberon-Greene, a single mother with two kids and three jobs, in a rundown mobile home painted barn red in the foothills of the Blue Ridge Mountains in north Georgia, five miles away from Helen and, thus, from civilization, as Amy had seen it in these parts of the woods, and three miles into the middle of nowhere.

The mobile home park was quiet midmorning on that Monday when Amy and Cyrus pulled up to the red house and parked outside, where an empty wooden doghouse sat rotting under a tree. All around the tree and the yard were rotting wood and cut branches, a veritable trash heap fit for burning.

*So it has come to this.*

The once great Walter Oberon, who had tried to buy Christmastown from Dad, who had slept with his best friend's wife and fathered a daughter, was now reduced to living in squalor.

As Amy dragged herself out of her rental car, she prayed for grace to deal with the circumstances that she had no control over.

"Remember." Cyrus's voice was a whisper, but Amy heard it in the thin air.

It wasn't nearly the fullness of fall yet in the southern USA, and one couldn't see the turning leaves until October, but the air bespoke a chill that loomed before them.

"Yes, I remember." She nodded. "The joy of the Lord is my strength."

The last part of Nehemiah 8:10 washed over her.

As they approached the front steps, a sudden clanging startled Amy. Then a crash. Then yelling and screaming.

All coming from inside that red box of a house.

She stopped. So did Cyrus.

"We don't have to do this," Cyrus said.

"You don't. I do."

When it quietened again, they continued walking to the front door. Amy pushed the doorbell, but the cracked button didn't move.

Cyrus rapped the wooden door with his

knuckles.

The door sounded hollow.

Footsteps approached from the other side.

Some kid screamed, "Mommy! Mommy!"

And Amy wanted to turn and run.

But the door swung open.

&

"*I* told her not to tell you!" Uncle Walt was beside himself—if he could be anywhere beside himself in his hospital bed that took up half the living room.

To his left and right were machines and contraptions.

In the center of it all, Uncle Walt looked like death. He could barely sit up.

*What in the world is wrong with Uncle Walt?*

"That woman!" he ranted on.

"Please don't speak like that about Mom," Amy said.

Yes, in spite of the twenty-eight years of lies, Rhoda Untermeyer was still Mom to her, Isaac, and Garrett.

Dad wasn't around anymore to protect Mom, so it was up to her children to make sure she was still respected, especially by this man who had messed up their family.

Then again, it took two to tango.

"Well, your lovely mom didn't listen. Told her to let me die in peace." Walt lifted up an arm. It had tubes connecting to it.

"I came on my own accord."

"How do you even know where I live?"

Amy didn't say that his daughter had visited her a few weeks before.

Speaking of whom, here she came with two dirty plastic cups, cracked on the rim, liquid inside, balanced precariously on a chipped tray.

"Water?" Meadow Lark offered.

"Thank you, but we just ate before we got here," Amy said.

Somewhere at the other end of the small space —probably only about eleven hundred square feet —a boy yelled, "Mommy! Hungry!"

Amy's heart broke.

Meadow Lark's face twitched, and she put the tray down. "Owen, we just ate!"

"I want another cookie!"

"We don't have cookies, stupid!" a little girl's voice screamed.

The high-pitched back and forth went on until Amy began to sway in the torn armchair that smelled like cigarette smoke or mold—or both. She tried to remember not to touch anything with her bare skin.

How could anyone live in such a dump?

Meadow Lark went to her dad and adjusted the pillow under his head, almost bald now.

"It's time for his dialysis," she said quietly.

Dialysis?

"They call this hemodialysis," Meadow Lark explained, emphasizing each syllable as if she had earned the right to use it. "We do it daily, and I've been trained."

"My daughter here is going to be a nurse someday," Uncle Walt added. "She's getting her GED and then will go from there."

The big machine and Uncle Walt connected, and Amy sat there watching tubes go in and out of his arm.

He closed his eyes. "I don't want you to see me like this."

He began to cry.

Amy had never seen Uncle Walt cry. Ever.

"Well, at least I'm not waiting for a heart," he said. "I'm waiting to die."

There was nothing more to be said.

Cyrus was so quiet that Amy almost forgot he was there, if he hadn't reached over and held her hand every now and then to remind her she was not alone.

Alone?

*Lord Jesus, have mercy on Uncle Walt.*

The visit ended when Uncle Walt fell asleep.

Amy had come to pay her respects to a dying man, and that was that.

She was ready to get out of here, drive straight home to Savannah, and hide in a hole somewhere.

Well, okay, not a hole—now that she had seen what a hole in the ground really looked like.

*Welcome to reality.*

Her childhood—rosy and pretty, warm and delightful—had been like a picture book of kids running around growing Christmas trees at the farm that Dad had named after her.

"All we need is snow," Isaac used to say, sometimes sticking his head into the freezer to see what it would feel like if Savannah had been snow country. Light dusting and thin layers of snow—and the rare blizzards—did not a white Christmas make.

Somehow Amy found herself looking up into the sky outside the mobile home. The sky was darkening. Rain would come.

Behind her and Cyrus, Meadow Lark slowly shut the door.

"Thank you for coming, Amy," she said. "It means a lot to Dad."

Amy barely nodded. Funny how it went. She couldn't make herself acknowledge that she could be somehow related to Uncle Walt. Seriously.

*I think we need a paternity test before we go*

*from here.*

Somehow in Amy's mind, she could not imagine how Uncle Walt could be her dad. They didn't look alike in any way. Not in mannerism, speech, whatever.

Amy was more like Felix Untermeyer.

He would always be Dad to her.

*No matter what the paternity test says.*

"Mom passed away a few years ago," Meadow Lark continued. "She and Dad had been together some forty years. After Mom died, Dad went downhill, and then he got diabetes, and now this."

This what? Amy didn't want to know, but she knew she was going to be told in the next second.

"Like I told you, Dad has end-stage renal disease, Miss Untermeyer."

Amy nodded.

"The nurse called again yesterday. There's still no match."

That, Amy didn't know.

"What about you?" Amy asked. "You're his daughter."

"I guess you couldn't have known. Mom already had me when she met Dad. They never had any children together."

Realization struck Amy.

This was why Meadow Lark had taken pains to find her.

She didn't know how to respond, what to say. All she wanted was to get out of there.

She glanced at Cyrus, who seemed to understand.

"We'd better get going. We have a long drive back to Savannah." Cyrus pointed to the low, dark clouds in the September sky. "Looks like it's going to rain."

Meadow Lark nodded. "Goodbye."

Amy wasn't sure if she wanted to say goodbye.

"You know, it's hard to find out your dad has a whole 'nother family. Does it feel weird to you?"

"I'm still trying to let it all sink in," Amy said. "My whole life I've thought my parents were madly in love with each other."

"Me too. To think that after they'd been married some twelve years, Dad cheated on Mom."

"And Mom cheated on Dad."

"You'd think that people who settled down after a dozen years would stop playing the field."

Amy said nothing.

"So let's see. I was thirteen when you were born."

Amy didn't want to go there. "We'll talk more later. Gotta run."

"Will you keep in touch?" Meadow Lark asked.

Amy half nodded.

# PART III

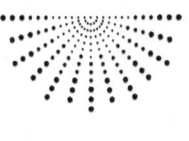

## JOY

# CHAPTER TWENTY-THREE

*A*my was sleeping soundly in her twin bed when her iPhone made a plinking sound at her. At first she thought it was part of her dream, until the plinking sounds became incessant.

She opened her eyes and surveyed the ceiling painted white.

Sabine from church had done a marvelous job turning the interior of this loft apartment into a small retreat for her. The nautical theme could be seen in the exposed beams above her all the way to the ocean-blue wainscoting all around her.

The apartment was sparsely furnished, just as Amy wanted, but here and there, on white-painted doors and rustic tables, seashell motifs and carved wooden seabirds reminded her that she was twenty minutes from the Atlantic Ocean.

On walls all around her, Amy's coastal photographs hung. These were from her own personal collection, which hadn't won any awards but the awards of the heart because Cyrus had helped her pick out what to put on the walls.

She had given him several of her framed photographs of Hawaii and Alaska to hang in his office at the Christmastown warehouse.

Her phone plinked again.

Amy reached for it on the distressed teal night-stand, feeling the pull in her waist. She flinched a little. Prayed for relief.

She tapped her iPhone screen.

*We're outside your door. Please open up.*

Cyrus.

Amy winced as she slowly got out of her bed.

It had been only a month, and she was healing up from the surgery. She didn't have the energy or emotional strength to go back to work this soon. She had decided to take the rest of the year off.

The good news was that, with Rasheed's help in finding a scheduling software that actually worked, Daisy was now able to efficiently schedule everyone at Amy's Destination Photography, placing them at the right location, at the right time, with no wasted days to spare.

In fact the whole thing had gone so well that nobody had asked for Amy.

That was the bad news.

Amy hadn't realized all the ramifications that would come by donating a kidney to Uncle Walt. Yes, to her, he would always be Uncle Walt, even though paternity tests had shown that they were not only related, but that she had a matching kidney to save his life.

Amy didn't want to consider the idea that God had allowed her to be born so that someday she could save her biological father's life on earth.

But Walt had listened to her when she spoke about Jesus before they went under the knife at Savannah Memorial.

Amy wanted to be sure that if they never awoke from their surgeries that Uncle Walt knew Jesus as his personal Lord and Savior and that his soul would wake up in heaven, regardless.

Uncle Walt had let her speak, but he didn't make a decision either way—whether to accept or reject Christ.

And now that they had both survived the surgeries, perhaps God would give Amy new opportunities to share Christ with Uncle Walt.

Amy reached the door as the thought alighted that perhaps she was too adult to call him Uncle Walt anymore.

Well, Cyrus still called his closest relatives Uncle Mel and Aunt Marie.

Amy looked through the peephole.

Cyrus was making faces at her.

She shook her head. *My boyfriend is an over-sized kid!*

She opened the door and was met with violin and guitar music flanking a trio wearing Christmas wreaths around their necks.

They flung into a medley of Christmas carols and hymns, and eventually ended with Amy's favorite: "O Holy Night."

When they finished their quick off-season caroling, Amy clapped.

"What's all this?" she asked, recognizing the guitarist and violinist from church. "It's only mid-November."

"Some options for our new family tradition," Cyrus said.

"Our?"

"Well, if you prefer, you can start your own. Next time we'll do option two. I'll be your Christmas tradition whisperer."

*Gag.* "What are we going to do without you, Cyrus?"

"Well, I'm always at your service, ma'am. And right now I see you're in your pajamas at ten in the morning. Your doctor's appointment is in thirty minutes."

"What? Today?"

"Uh-huh. And what are you going to do without me, Amy?"

# CHAPTER TWENTY-FOUR

*T*he doctor's visit went well. Amy should be well by Christmas. Woo—

*Ouch.*

She still felt pain where the laparoscope surgery had made little incisions here and there. She had been told the recovery period was about six to eight weeks, and she had been advised to give herself three months to completely heal.

But no way was she going back to Mom's house after that first month of being overly pampered by Mom. Still, she enjoyed sleeping in her old bed at the house.

Thank God that Mom had changed her mind about selling the Untermeyer family home. She decided that there was more backyard space in that house than there was at the Savannah Senior

Living Resort. Her grandkids could run around when they came over to visit.

*Grandkids?*

None of Amy's siblings had kids.

Yet.

The only people she could think of who might go over to Mom's house were Jerome's two grandchildren from Tamsyn and Ryan. What a cute couple they were, and they had produced two cute girls.

Mom hadn't said much about her engagement with Jerome, but they were still going out with each other.

"A cupcake for your thoughts?" Cyrus asked.

Amy said nothing.

"You didn't like us caroling at ten in the morning?"

"Not that."

"Then what?"

"I'm not pulling my fair share at Christmastown," Amy said.

"You're recovering from surgery." Cyrus cruised to a stop in front of the old tavern—and future photography studio—that Amy had bought.

"I should've been able to get back to work in six weeks, but I'm not."

"There'll be plenty of work for you to do. Don't

worry." Cyrus smiled. "Besides, you can't fly out of the country anyway."

Amy opened the car door. "Christmas will be over by the time I'm healed."

"Inventory is never over. Besides, our busiest time of January is when we take down all the decorations and box up everything."

Amy nodded.

"Right now, a lot of the work is heavy lifting, climbing on ladders, carrying trees, and so forth," Cyrus reminded her. "We've hired some able-bodied college students who didn't leave town for Christmas. They're getting extra pay, extra spending money. Let them work."

Amy nodded again.

"If you want, you could come to the office and do some office work," Cyrus suggested.

"I want to."

"I'll pick you up in the morning then."

"Thank you, Cy." Amy stepped out of the car and spotted someone standing outside her soon-to-be photography studio.

*Oh yes.* "My interior designer is here. I need to go over some design plans with her."

"See what I mean? You keep busy. And you might as well ask her to give you some ideas for your loft apartment."

"Sure. Why not?"

# CHAPTER TWENTY-FIVE

*N*ovember was the beginning of the end on Cyrus's calendar. This was the period that he called Emergency Christmas. It was when people realized that Christmas was about a month away and they hadn't gotten anything done.

It was the onset of decorating panic.

"So they outsource it all to Christmastown," Cyrus explained to Amy across from the lunch table in the break room.

He had purposely picked up Amy late this morning so that she had a short first day back at work. Amy hadn't complained. To keep her from exerting herself, he quickly ushered her into a business meeting.

"How can anyone outsource Christmas?" Amy asked. "This is exactly what I'm fighting against."

"Hold on. Before your pine needles start shaking off the tree, hear me out." Cyrus spread his palm on the steel table. "We take the stress out of their decorating woes. We help them focus on what's important to them—hopefully God and family."

Amy waved a brochure in the air. "How does this play into the plan?"

"It's a menu. They choose how much they want us to help them. Maybe some even need a caterer or a personal chef. We have partners we can call. Like Piper's Place, for example. They could cater."

"Okay."

"How many home cooks are chained to their kitchen stoves all day long—some for days— preparing Christmas meals and dishes they're the last people to taste?"

"For a price."

"We all win. We get a profit." Cyrus was confident of it. "The customer gets peace of mind."

"You want me to approve this." Amy studied the brochure again, filled with checklists of a la carte Christmas preparation options.

"They can go online also."

"Why this last-minute addition?"

"To boost sales. Reach beyond our corporate customers."

"When did this bright idea appear?"

"We just thought of it last week. Me and Rasheed." Cyrus had wanted to include Amy in the brainstorming, but he didn't want to put any undue stress on her.

In fact, while he had agreed to let Amy come to the office to do light work, he had asked all fifty-plus employees of Christmastown to keep an eye on her. If she as much as sneezed or coughed, he wanted to be told.

She had done a selfless act of giving a kidney to a man who didn't care one way or another. Now she must get well. Heal.

Cyrus knew that Amy was not a hundred percent yet. He didn't want her in the warehouse, but he didn't want her to think she was being rejected.

On the contrary, he cared too much.

"Tell me one thing." Amy put down the paper. "You're doing everything for everyone else. What are you doing for you at Christmas?"

*What does she mean?* "I'm happy to serve."

"Glad you found your joy."

"Amy."

"What?" She looked up.

*How do I remind her?*

153

"My joy is in the Lord, remember? Not in the things I do. Don't get me wrong. I'm happy with my job and ministry. Serving God is my calling. But I don't seek joy through service. My joy is secure in the Lord regardless of whether I get to serve or not."

Cyrus reached across the table and held Amy's hands. "I wish you joy, Amy. No matter what goes on in life, I wish you joy in the Lord always."

# CHAPTER TWENTY-SIX

Sure enough, Amy had found something to do for the next five weeks. The joy of the Lord carried through a quiet Thanksgiving with Mom, just the two of them. Cyrus was with Uncle Mel and Aunt Marie. Jerome was with Tamsyn and Ryan.

Right after Thanksgiving, Amy felt better. Mom invited her to stay at the old house while her photography studio and loft apartment were being renovated. Amy had to say yes. The construction dust alone would cover all her furniture, not to mention her clothes, and maybe even her lungs.

So back to Mom's house she went.

They rarely spoke about Uncle Walt except when an update came in from Meadow Lark.

Walt was getting better. Color had returned to

his face. The hemodialysis machine was gone. Slowly, he was able to get out of the house and sit outside in the yard. He also walked to the mailbox and back.

By the time the twelve days of Christmas came, Christmastown was fully booked, and Cyrus was doing the work of twelve men.

"So we decorate houses and businesses for people, and we come here for our Christmas Eve dinner?" Amy asked as she stepped into Piper's Place.

"It's a tradition," Uncle Mel said, wheeling Aunt Marie in. She simply smiled.

"A new tradition," Cyrus said, stealing a kiss as Amy walked by him holding the door.

Up the elevator they went to the third floor, where Amy could hear ensemble music—soft and lovely and Christmas themed. Next to the Christmas-red baby grand piano, a quartet filled the string section with two violins, a cello, and a harp.

On both sides of the musicians and instruments were clusters of fake pine trees of varying heights.

The server led them to a long table that could easily seat twelve people.

Amy's eyebrows lifted when she saw the people at the table.

A beaming Meadow Lark and her two children

dressed so colorfully they could compete with the decor in the room, and Uncle Walt, looking alive again, sitting on the other side of the kids, chatting with Mom and Jerome Pendegrast like they were old friends.

And they had been.

*A long time ago when Dad...*

*The joy of the Lord is my strength.*

Amy sniffled. Her only wish was for her two brothers to be here with them. She glanced back at the elevator door, just in case it opened and out came Isaac and Garrett.

No such thing.

The elevator door remained shut.

Christmas dinner was simply roast turkey with cranberry sauce, with delightful house stuffing that was a signature side dish at Piper's Place. Nothing they hadn't eaten before, except this time, Amy watched in merriment as the two kids—Owen and Samantha—oohed and aahed at every single helping of food their mom put on their plates.

Before desert came, Cyrus leaned over toward Amy and gently kissed her cheek. Then he whispered something in her ear.

"Will you marry me?"

It was so soft Amy almost didn't hear the words. And it was done so low key she had missed Uncle Walt's silly jokes.

"Pardon?" She turned to ask, but Cyrus was not in his seat.

He was at the red piano. A soft medley of Christmas music floated up from the piano.

"I didn't know he could play the piano." Mom gasped.

"I didn't either," Amy said.

Across the table, Uncle Mel beamed. "Marie taught him a long time ago. Nice to know he hasn't forgotten."

Amy turned her attention back to Cyrus.

He was looking directly at her as the soft Christmas music ebbed away into a tune that Amy didn't recognize. Cyrus began to sing but only five words.

"Amy, will you marry me?"

# CHAPTER TWENTY-SEVEN

*W*ithout a word, Amy walked as fast as she could, hobbling at the edge of pain in her side, toward the elevator.

The door closed as she saw Cyrus get up slowly from the piano bench, his face looking stunned.

When the door reopened on the first floor of Piper's Place, she wove through the restaurant crowd, down the hallway, and out the door into the frigid December night under the twinkling Savannah skies that had been there for thousands of years.

The sidewalk was cold.

The wall was cold.

The air was cold.

She heard the Piper's Place front door open to

her right, and there was Cyrus, stepping out and coming toward her. In one of his hands was her winter coat.

She rested her head against the brick wall and closed her eyes.

"I didn't mean to scare you," Cyrus spoke quietly.

Amy opened her eyes to find Cyrus leaning against the wall, his face very close to hers. He didn't touch her.

She took her coat from him and put it on. "Thanks."

"It's cold out here."

"I wasn't scared," she whispered.

"Terrified?"

"No. Just startled."

"I guess you were so startled that you leapt out of your seat and flew out of the third floor."

Amy grimaced. Her side hurt a bit. "It wasn't that dramatic. I think I barely hobbled."

She willed her heart to calm down.

Could she spend the rest of her life on earth with this Christmas dude? They'd talk Christmas year round.

"What about Easter?" she asked.

"Well... We could get married around Easter time, but I'd rather keep that sacred time of year focused on the death, burial, and resurrection of Jesus Christ."

"That's not what I was asking."

Cyrus leaned closer. "What are you asking? Thinking?"

"Are we going to talk Christmas year round?"

"We run Christmastown. We might not be able to help ourselves."

"I think we need to expand the company. I would like to do charity work..."

"Amy, we can discuss the direction of our company, but..." Cyrus produced an engagement ring from his pocket. It sparkled a bit under the streetlight. "But this is not a business proposal, you know. You're not marrying Christmastown. Let's talk about the company later, all right? This is more personal."

Before she could say a word, he embraced her, cheek to cheek.

"I want to spend the rest of my life with you, Amy Untermeyer," he said. "Marry, marry me? Please?"

"Because?"

"Because I love you."

Amy cupped his face in her cold hands. "I love you too, Cyrus."

He slipped the ring onto her finger and sealed

their promise with a kiss so long and enduring that Amy forgot to breathe.

"We can go anywhere for our honeymoon. Know why?" There was cheer in his voice.

"Why?"

"I have a passport now."

"Seriously?" Amy hugged him tightly.

"Yep. Now I have to go *somewhere*."

"You do?"

"As long as I'm with you."

"Hmm... You know, we can't travel all the time, living out of suitcases, raising a family at airports." Amy played with her engagement ring. It was a bit loose, but they'd resize it later. "I'm warming up to the idea of staycations."

"That's my girl!"

# CHAPTER TWENTY-EIGHT

*C*yrus thanked God that Amy had ironed out the schedule at Amy's Destination Photography. With the new system she had installed, efficiency was not only in place, but Amy was able to hire two new photographers out of the Savannah College of Art and Design. They were young, talented, and were ready to travel around the world.

By April, Amy's Studio on River Street, now the base camp of all her photography ventures, had opened for business.

Down the street, Simon's Gallery had also offered to showcase some of her award-winning photographs and bridal magazine covers.

And Mrs. U and Amy—their relationship still raw and delicate—had been able to come together through photography. It was a neutral ground where they could talk and get along most of the time. There was a truce between mother and daughter. Amy had hired her mother to be one of her principal photographers at Amy's Studio.

It showed Cyrus how selfless Amy was.

*And now, here we are.*

He and Amy had considered marrying on the riverboat where Riverside Chapel held its Sunday services, but decided they wanted a more intimate location than River Street, only the most famous area in Savannah.

Jerome Pendegrast had found them a small chapel inside a private home in a quieter residential neighborhood, away from the touristy downtown.

It was just what Cyrus and Amy wanted. The mansion was no more than fifteen minutes away from Riverside Chapel, and wedding guests were able to find parking spaces around the squares outside the property.

Cyrus could hear the music playing on the other side of the wall as he adjusted his bow tie in the mirror in a room that looked more like a closet.

He threw on his tuxedo jacket and spun around. "How do I look?"

"Never better." Rasheed was sitting down at a narrow window, checking his iPad. Saturday morning sunlight was on his hair, and it looked like he was graying on top.

Silently, Cyrus prayed for his relationship with Amy. He knew without a doubt that Amy was the one whom God had brought into his life to be his wife.

But going forth, all those weeks of premarital counseling at Riverside Chapel had to bear fruit.

For the rest of their lives.

# CHAPTER TWENTY-NINE

"*N*o weeping, Amy. No weeping." Mom handed Amy another wad of tissue paper.

"Yikes. Now we have to redo my eyes all over again." Amy looked in the mirror and saw bits of mascara on top of her cheek.

The makeup artist simply smiled. Perhaps she had seen such things before. She set out to repair the damage.

Amy held back another tear as she sat amid a flurry of activities all around her. Someone was pinning all over her hair.

Midori was here and there, snapping pictures every two seconds or so.

Amy closed her eyes and prayed that God would hold her up. All she had to do was last for two hours, and then all this makeup could come off, and her hair could be unpinned, and she could throw on a comfortable tee shirt and a pair of old shorts.

Then she could let it all out.

*I wish Dad were here.*

And Isaac.

And Garrett.

Her half sister was out there sitting next to Uncle Walt. He had refused to be asked to walk Amy down the aisle.

"You'll always be Felix's daughter, never mine. He will always be your father."

*Well, thanks.*

So.

Nobody was going to give Amy away today.

She sighed. Someone tapped her shoulder.

She closed her eyes.

Jerome Pendegrast had volunteered to walk her down the aisle. Seriously? The man was kind, but no. Amy hardly knew him, except as Tamsyn's dad from long ago. And now, as Mom's fiancé—

Her future stepfather.

Someone tapped her shoulder again.

"What?"

She opened her eyes and—

Shrieked!

"Isaac!"

*Will you all please stop startling me like this?*

She remembered how Cyrus had sneaked up on her at the Ecola State Park. That was a treat. And now—

"You're here! You're here!" She jumped up and down and up and down. "Isaac is herree...!"

"Hey, little sister, how you doing?" Isaac spoke calmly, like it was no big deal that his sister was overly excited to see him.

Amy bear-hugged him. "I'm so fine now that you're here."

"I have a surprise for you."

"You *are* the surprise!"

Isaac stepped aside.

And Amy gasped. "Garrett?"

Her knees went weak as she crossed the rug toward her other brother. He was clean shaven, tanned. Like an apparition.

Amy stuck out a finger and pressed his chest. "Garrett?"

"You look so pretty."

And she burst into tears, hugged Garrett so tightly, and couldn't let him go.

When she finally composed herself, Amy glanced over to find Mom crying quietly by the mirror. In a few strides—and without tripping over her lace wedding gown—Amy reached Mom.

Her brothers followed in a group hug.

In that moment, Amy hoped that Dad would be pleased with them, that they had finally reunited as a family—albeit late, when it could only be in his loving memory.

In her heart, Amy prayed that God would lead them forward, as the future was most certainly in His perfect hands.

# CHAPTER THIRTY

The processional was delayed by at least fifteen minutes as the poor makeup lady scrubbed all the smeared makeup off Amy's face a third time, reapplied her eyeshadow, and then ushered her out the door before something else happened.

When the pretty harp music began a hymn arrangement of praise to God, Amy beamed with joy as both her brothers walked her down the aisle.

*Thank You, Lord Jesus. Thank You. Thank you.*

The look on Cyrus's face was priceless when he saw Amy's brothers bringing her down the aisle toward him.

Amy liked to think that her brothers were her protectors. They had always been when she was little. Now they were all back again, from different parts of the world.

Pretty soon, everyone would have to go back to work. But for now, she had her entire family with her, even Mom, poor Mom, who had gone through so much in her life.

Except Dad.

Amy would like to think that Dad was smiling and rejoicing with her while he was enjoying his eternal life with Jesus in heaven.

Someday, when it was time to go, she would see Dad again.

Until then, there was work to be done.

A wedding to complete.

A marriage to live out with the man whom she loved.

Amy reached the platform, where Pastor Flores stood with Cyrus and his best man, Rasheed.

Eventually, Pastor Flores reached the big question. "Who gives this woman to be married to this man?"

"We and her mother do," Garrett and Isaac said in unison.

Amy was impressed. She grinned. But she didn't want to let go of her brothers' strong arms.

They both leaned down to kiss her on her cheeks.

Isaac whispered in her ear. "Go to your husband. I have to check the kitchen to be sure your reception is perfect."

*Once a chef, always a chef.*

Amy found herself laughing out loud.

Cyrus furrowed his brows, not being privy to the joke between brother and sister.

To Garrett, Amy mouthed, *I love you so much.*

His eyes glistened.

Amy let go of her brothers' arms. Cyrus was there to help her up the platform.

He was there still, holding her hand throughout the wedding ceremony.

And Amy knew that he would be there for the rest of their lives together as husband and wife.

## GOD'S WORD IS SWEETER THAN HONEY

## FAREWELL FROM AMY AND CYRUS

Then he said unto them, Go your way, eat the fat, and drink the sweet, and send portions unto them for whom nothing is prepared: for this day is holy unto our Lord: neither be ye sorry; for the joy of the Lord is your strength.

— NEHEMIAH 8:10

And the angel said unto them, Fear not: for, behold, I bring you good tidings of great joy, which shall be to all people. For unto you is born this day in the city of David a Saviour, which is Christ the Lord.

— LUKE 2:10-11

Thank you for reading *Wish You Joy*. If you enjoyed the story of Amy and Cyrus, would you please write a review? Reviews are helpful to other readers. The book page on my website lists the retailer links where you can post your reviews, if you wish:

Wish You Joy (Savannah Sweethearts Book 9)
JanThompson.com/wish

Subscribe to my newsletter to receive book news updates and special book sales. Be notified when my new books are available.

Jan Thompson's Mailing List:
JanThompson.com/newsletter

Are you new to Savannah Sweethearts ? *Know You More* is the first book in this series of clean and wholesome Christian romances set in Savannah and on Tybee Island.

Know You More (Savannah Sweethearts Book 1)
JanThompson.com/know

After *Wish You Joy*, the next book in the Savannah Sweethearts series is *Call You Home* (Savannah Sweethearts Book 10).

Continue reading for a preview of *Call You Home*.

THE NEXT BOOK IS CALL
YOU HOME

SAVANNAH SWEETHEARTS BOOK 10

*Is he one chef too many in her kitchen?*
*Will she fire him before he is even hired?*

After *Wish You Joy*, the next and final book in the Savannah Sweethearts series is *Call You Home* (Savannah Sweethearts Book 10). We return to Piper's Place, the café frequented by Riverside Chapel church members.

Do you remember restaurateur Piper Peyton? She has made cameo appearances in the series, particularly in *Know You More* (Savannah Sweethearts Book 1).

In *Call You Home*, we visit Piper's busy kitchen to see if there are too many cooks. How long will Chef Isaac Untermeyer last?

⁂

*Call You Home* will be coming soon. Sign up for Jan Thompson's mailing List to receive notification when this book is available.

To be notified when *Call You Home* is available:
JanThompson.com/newsletter

Call You Home (Savannah Sweethearts Book 10):
JanThompson.com/call

Savannah Sweethearts:
JanThompson.com/savannah

# ACKNOWLEDGMENTS

Many thanks to my Georgia Press publishing team for keeping up with my writing schedule.

For this book, I thank my outstanding copyeditor, Dori Harrell, and my patient proofreader, Lenda Selph. Their eyes for details are from the Lord.

I also want to thank my husband and son for their constant support and encouragement. And my parents for instilling in me the love to read and write at a very early age.

Most of all, I am eternally thankful to my Lord and Savior, Jesus Christ, who died on the cross to save me from my sins and rose again from the grave to give me eternal life. Without Him, I can write and do nothing.

Jan Thompson
John 3:16

# ARE YOU ON JAN THOMPSON'S MAILING LIST?

Are you on *USA Today* bestselling author Jan Thompson's mailing list? Get book release news, sales and special deals, promotional notifications, and behind-the-scene-information about her books.

Keep up with Jan as she writes more books for you to enjoy.

Subscribe to Jan's Mailing List:
JanThompson.com/newsletter

BOOKS BY JAN THOMPSON

CONTEMPORARY CHRISTIAN ROMANCE &
ROMANTIC WOMEN'S FICTION

**Savannah Sweethearts** (11 Books)
JanThompson.com/savannah

**Vacation Sweethearts** (5 Books)
JanThompson.com/vacation

**Seaside Chapel** (9 Books)
JanThompson.com/seaside

CHRISTIAN ROMANTIC SUSPENSE

**Protector Sweethearts** (6 Books)
JanThompson.com/protector

**Binary Hackers** (3 Books)
JanThompson.com/binary

**(Sister Series to Binary Hackers)**
*Coming Soon*

SAVANNAH SWEETHEARTS
(CONTEMPORARY CHRISTIAN ROMANCE)

JanThompson.com/savannah

- Book 0: Ask You Later (Prequel)
- Book 1: Know You More
- Book 2: Tell You Soon (Romance with Suspense)
- Book 3: Draw You Near
- Book 4: Cherish You So
- Book 5: Walk You There
- Book 6: Love You Always (Romance with Suspense)
- Book 7: Kiss You Now
- Book 8: Find You Again
- Book 9: Wish You Joy (Christmas Romance)
- Book 10: Call You Home

Meet a group of multiethnic churchgoing Christians who love the Lord, work hard in their careers, and seek God's will for their love lives.

Against a backdrop of ocean, sand, and sun, these inspirational romances showcase aspects of the human need for God and for one another.

Have some tea, settle on a comfortable reading

chair, and enjoy these sweet celebrations of faith, hope, and love in Jesus Christ.

## VACATION SWEETHEARTS (CONTEMPORARY CHRISTIAN ROMANCE)

JanThompson.com/vacation

- Book 1: Smile for Me
- Book 2: Reach for Me (Romance with Suspense)
- Book 3: Wait for Me
- Book 4: Look for Me
- Book 5: Cheer for Me

Travel with our friends from Savannah, Georgia, to the coast and to the mountains. Cheer them on as they celebrate the immeasurable grace and undeserved mercy of God through Jesus Christ.

The Vacation Sweethearts novels are a spin-off of Jan's Savannah Sweethearts series, and fans will recognize familiar faces from Riverside Chapel, a church in the coastal city of Savannah, Georgia.

In fact, we might even visit the beach town of Tybee Island from time to time to visit old friends and beloved families...

The collection begins with *Smile for Me,* the story of Byron Moss and Tina MacFarland, spending their summer on the Caribbean islands of the Bahamas where the water is blue and hearts are warm...

## SEASIDE CHAPEL (CONTEMPORARY CHRISTIAN ROMANCE & ROMANTIC WOMEN'S FICTION)

JanThompson.com/seaside

- Book 1: Share with Me
- Book 2: Step with Me
- Book 3: Sing with Me
- (More Books to Come)

The novels of Seaside Chapel blend women's fiction with contemporary Christian romance to celebrate the grace of God and hope in Jesus Christ.

Visit Jan's favorite beach town of St. Simon's Island, Georgia, where our friends live and attend Seaside Chapel, a little church by the sea known for its beach weddings and fair shares of love and life.

As these Christians grow in their knowledge and understanding of God, they are tested in their spiritual maturity, their relationships with others, and their love lives. Share their heartaches and healing, and cheer them on as they celebrate faith, family, friends, and yes, happily-ever-afters.

The Seaside Chapel novels are all about life by the Atlantic Ocean, which in essence, is not much different from life in landlocked cities. Inherently, the human nature is such that we have in our hearts a need for the Lord, for His salvation, sustenance, and sanctification.

## PROTECTOR SWEETHEARTS (CHRISTIAN ROMANTIC SUSPENSE)

JanThompson.com/protector

- Book 1: Once a Thief
- Book 2: Once a Hero
- Book 3: Once a Spy
- (More Books to Come)

Protector Sweethearts is a spinoff of Savannah Sweethearts. Protector Sweethearts begins with Book 1 (Once a Thief), Private Investigator Helen Hu's story.

Helen makes cameo appearances in *Tell You Soon* (Savannah Sweethearts Book 2) and *Step with Me* (Seaside Chapel Book 2). Helen is petite and feisty. And then there's Mama Hu, the one with all those secrets causing commotions...

BINARY HACKERS (INSPIRATIONAL ROMANTIC THRILLER)

JanThompson.com/binary

- Book 1: Zero Sum
- Book 2: Zero Day
- Book 3: Zero Base

Binary Hackers is a Christian romantic suspense series, featuring the employees of Binary Systems, a computer security company in Atlanta, Georgia.

It is set in the same story world as Jan Thompson's other books, and characters from the other series may make cameo appearances in Binary Hackers.

This series is actually a prequel to another series coming soon, but we'll talk about that later...

## ABOUT JAN THOMPSON

*USA Today* bestselling author Jan Thompson writes multiethnic Christian fiction that celebrates the grace and mercy of God with hope and love in Jesus Christ.

From wholesome Christian romance with flavors of women's fiction to clean Christian romantic suspense and inspirational international thrillers, Jan's books are for readers who enjoy stories of faith, family, friends, and yes, happy endings. Always.

Find out more about Jan Thompson:
JanThompson.com

Subscribe to Jan's mailing list for book news:
JanThompson.com/newsletter

*For God so loved the world,*
*that He gave His only begotten Son,*
*that whosoever believeth in Him should not perish,*
*but have everlasting life.*
—John 3:16